TOUGH AS OLD BOOTS

Book Two of the "Never Too Old" Western Series

J.V. JAMES

Classic West Tales

DEDICATION

to our tough old boy, Toots

CONTENTS

CHAPTER 1
LEAP'N'ROLL
AUGUST, 1878. SANTA MONICA, CALIFORNIA.

Into the pleasant morning they came, whooping and hollering into our bliss, a family Saturday meal on the porch of our home.

Their blood-curdling shrieks pierced the air — weren't just one or two riders, but a whole wild bunch all urging their mounts on, the old sound of death on their lips.

The words *"Inside now"* tumble out of me, and not a moment too soon.

As my girls disappear through the house's side doorway, a lone bullet sings through the air, smashes Georgina's teapot — and the scalding dark liquid explodes all over the table as I hit the deck.

"Lyle Frakes," comes the grizzled voice of a hard case, as the riders halt two-hundred yards off. "You killed our cousins in Custer City. Prepare now to die, you old coot."

Old? I HATE being called old.

I peer around the edge of the heavy log chair I'd been

sat on, and see the whole gang, spread out side by side, and all laughing.

One against six — reckon that scores us 'bout even once I get inside, so I best get busy.

I half-roll half-leap through the house's side doorway, yell to Georgina and Mary to "Get out the way, into that back room and stay there."

And Gertrude — that lovely old rifle who's been my good friend for so long — just about jumps from her place on the wall and snaps into position, already aimed at the lead rider as he spurs his horse forward.

Old am I then, you young cuss?
Let's see what old means.

CHAPTER 2
IF RIFLES COULD SMILE

I f rifles could smile, ol' Gertrude would have done so right then.

When I had this house built, I made sure there was small slots for rifles, one in each outside wall — battlements, one word you might call them — right at my comfortable eye height for shooting intruders.

Georgina didn't much like it — reckoned we'd made our new start, left that sorta life in the past — but some things ain't up for discussion, so I did what I wanted.

Now, me and Gertrude, we weren't in no hurry as them six riders came on. One rode wild and shrieked like a madman, way out ahead of the others and waving his pistol, right in our sights. Determined to die young, I guess — some fellers is like that.

Two-hundred yards off when he spurred his horse into action; then one-eighty, one-sixty, one-forty, my finger now warm on the trigger.

One-twenty yards off now, I'm commencing to squeeze — but just as I fired, that battle-crazed lead feller's horse turned, and I heard some new horses a'coming.

Gertrude's bullet sang its terrible tune at the very same moment all six riders turned to their right. And also, two new riders hot in pursuit, this pair shooting uselessly at the intruders from too far away.

Gertrude's bullet tore into the lead man — his arm I believe; but no, it must have smashed into his torso, for he fell from his horse as it wheeled around, and the man hit the dirt, rolled once then stayed right where he landed — face down he was, didn't move.

His friends sure burned the breeze, galloping some pretty fine horseflesh across my front paddock and into the trees — a distance of a half-mile — while two-hundred yards behind *them* came the two new arrivals. Both these men made noise with their six-guns, despite being well out of range.

Why don't they take out their rifles? Not easy, I guess, at a gallop. Not easy for SOME anyway.

I was out of range too, so I waited.

Waited and watched.

Picked up my spyglass from its shelf right beside me.

Looked through it, waited some more.

A feller gets good at waiting — at least he does, if he hopes to survive.

So I waited right where I was, kept an oversize eye on proceedings — no sense in going outside 'til I find out who's who, that's a trap for young players.

The feller who'd crashed to the ground on my driveway still hadn't moved none at all. His horse showed no loyalty to him, chased its five friends into the trees, and now disappeared from my view, swallowed up by the forest. They had made straight for the best path, the one I sometimes rode up the hill — seemed to me like they already knew it was there, way they made a beeline right for it.

As for the two men doing the chasing, they went only as far as the tree-line — should have stopped sooner really, took cover, in case the whole thing was a trap and them killers was lying in wait.

It's what I'd have expected them five skunks to do.

But the two men went unaccosted. They turned their horses about, rode slowly back toward the dead man now — *probably dead, I should say.*

Always best to be certain.

As I watched through the spyglass, it was clear that both newcomers' horses were spent, their necks and forelegs flecked with foam from being hard ridden too far.

I saw then that one of those fellers was our own Town Marshal — recognizable by his pear shape, the man was paunchy and pudgy, a pen-pushing type of perhaps twenty-five, name of Rollins. Not exactly *my* type of lawman, but then, I got pretty high standards — and also, a preference for men who choose to serve *justice,* not the letter of the law. Seems to me that the letter of the law can often be wrong — but that's the way most do their Sheriffin', these modern times.

"Georgina, it's safe to come out," I called, without taking my eye from the spyglass. "Samuel Rollins and some other feller chased the men off, excepting for one lying still on the ground. I reckon that one's dead or dying. Both of you stay in the house while I sort it all out."

"One of them called you Lyle Frakes," said Georgina, as she and Mary hurried into the parlor, holding hands and looking more worried than they had since we'd come to this place a year back. "Oh, Kit, they know who you *really* are."

"They're cousins to those awful Prewitts," said Mary, her eyes worried, yet shining I noticed.

Child enjoys the excitement.

"That ain't necessarily true, Mary Farmer," I said.

"They must be, they said Custer City, I heard them. Father, I'm certain it's—"

"Stay right here," I said sharply. *"Both* of you. I'll go deal with this. If I do bring these two men inside, don't admit my name's Frakes. We'll discuss all that after they leave."

"They broke my good teapot, we'll just go out and clean—"

"No, Georgina," I growled, turning toward them, and putting the spyglass into my pocket. "You won't. You *won't*. Not yet anyway, stay inside. Please."

They glared at me, woman and child, but neither one spoke.

Me and Gertrude slipped out the heavy front door, and I closed it tight shut behind me. I knew what both my girls' faces must look like, their frosty silence still loud in my ears as I covered the distance toward the still body, roundabout ninety yards off.

Gertrude kept herself pointed at the man on the ground, despite how dead he looked. *She don't like surprises, ol' Gertrude.*

Still, she mighta been right — there was *something* about him that suggested aliveness. Sure enough, from thirty yards off I saw he was breathing — and not in short bursts like a feller who's dying, but shallow and slow, more-or-less like a man sleeping.

Only shot in the arm, like I thought. Still, most likely pretending. Best keep an eye on him.

I glanced at Town Marshal Rollins and his new friend, who got close to the man just as I did. Saw a flash of that new feller's badge on his shirt when his coat fell open a little.

"No need to point your rifle at a dead man," Rollins chuckled. "You killed him once already, Mister *Farmer.*"

Something in how he said *Farmer* set my nerves all a'jangle.

"The man's alive, Marshal Rollins," his smooth-voiced friend said as he dismounted, six-gun in hand, also pointed and ready.

He used his foot to roll the unconscious man over, but it was a powerful deep sleep that young feller was in. His eyes did not so much as flutter.

"Funny," the new lawman said, looking closely. "There aren't any marks on his head, but he must have hit hard to still be unconscious this long."

"If you say so," I answered, keeping Gertrude still aimed at the feller.

Smooth-Voice nodded to me then and said, "You know what to do, sir." Then he eased back the hammer of his six-gun and holstered it. Perhaps only twenty years old, he was what some folks might call a *pretty-boy,* a whole lot too handsome for Law work. Yet each of his movements was sharp and deliberate — and despite his youth, he knew *what* he was doing, and *why.* He went to the rear of the unconscious man, sat him up, pulled his hands behind his back.

Well, that poor shot feller sure squealed. His eyes opened wide as a man who's struck gold, he looked right at me and yelled, *"Frakes!"* Then he passed out unconscious again, his young chin on his chest.

I knew now that shot feller weren't acting — and hadn't hit his head neither. I had seen men like this twice before in my long career — men who could not withstand pain, and passed out whenever it struck.

As the sound of my real name hung there between us, Smooth-Voice looked up at me, raised up his eyebrows, and a slight smile played at his lips.

He knows too, dammit.

I stuck to my plan — such as it was — and, feigning surprise I said, "Who the hell's Franks?" Then I went on the front foot, got all accusatory at 'em. "Forget who Franks is, I don't care. More important, what are *you* two fellers playin' at, chasing killers onto my place? We was just partaking of lunch, and we coulda been killed."

"You don't understand, Mister Farmer," said Rollins.

"These men came here to kill *you!* This man here with me's a United States Marshal, and we rode hell for leather to save you, just look at our horses."

I could clearly see the badge pinned to the young feller's vest, his coat now being open.

"I'm only a Deputy Marshal," said Smooth-Voice, as he finished tying the unconscious man's hands. Then he gently laid the feller down in the dirt, stood and offered me his own hand to shake. "United States Deputy Marshal Lucas Golden at your service, sir. Please call me Luke — all my friends do."

Well, I sure weren't his friend. My friends mostly ain't *young,* and they surely ain't *overly handsome* — and this sparkle-eyed, wet-behind-the-ears U.S. Deputy was *both.* I reluctantly shook the offered hand, nodded a curt one at him and said, "Deputy Golden it is then. And I'm Kit Farmer."

"Bad way to begin, sir," he said. "Starting up with a lie."

I looked that Deputy hard in his sparkly eyes, but he never so much as flinched — not even when I used my quietest, most menacing voice and said, "Reckon I must not have heard right. Coulda swore you just called me a liar, young pup."

"I've tracked this gang all the way from Cheyenne, sir," he said, and his voice had a tone of respect now, so I let him keep speaking. "They've kept two steps ahead of me most of the way, killed a half-dozen men that I know of, and done worse to women. They've come a long way in order to do just one thing, sir. And that's to kill you — *you* — the famous Lyle Frakes."

I looked all the way in his eyes. Didn't flinch, and neither did he. And I said, "Lyle *who?*"

And he says, "Please, Mister Frakes, you're embarrassing yourself. We both know who you really are. You can stop lying now."

CHAPTER 3
"MOCK MY HORSE...?"

I didn't hit the uppity fool.

Then I didn't hit him *again*.

Wrathy as I was at how things had turned out — and smug as the look on that Deputy's handsome young face was — I knew it weren't really *his* fault, the way things had gone.

Still, I had hopes to turn this around yet — deal with the would-be killers in my own way, and still keep my reputation as quiet old *'Kit Farmer from Kansas.'*

So I laughed. Laughed it up big and hearty. Laughed right in that young feller's face.

"You think *I'm* Lyle Frakes, do you, son? Reckon you must be cracked. Oh, I know who he is. Met him once even. Truth is, I disliked the man. Weren't game to say so, a'course, given his reputation for meanness and violent short temper." I shook my head and laughed it up again before adding, *"Lyle dang Frakes* — ha, wait 'til I tell my wife, and she finds out who she married!"

"Mister Frakes, let me explain," said the young pup —
at least he was being persistent, as a good lawman should be.

"I'll give you half a minute, I got things to do, son. *Ha!*
Lyle dang Frakes, that's a good one! Just wait til I tell my
daughter, and she tells all her friends. Why, we'll be famous
all over town. *Lyle dang Frakes!*"

"The truth is, Mister Frakes, sir, I knew you were here,
perhaps even before the Prewitt Gang did. I have access to
more resources than they do, of course — *all* government
information is available to me, *if* it pertains to a case I'm
assigned to."

"Per-whatted? You'd best keep your talk simple, young
feller, I lack your fancy book-learnin'. Clear and simple,
y'hear?"

"How's this for *simple* then, sir? Lyle Frakes
disappeared from Cheyenne, just about the same day Kit
Farmer appeared. Oh, your friend in Cheyenne did a fair
enough job to help you disappear—"

"I went to Cheyenne once, but I ain't got friends there,
so I have no idea who you—"

"Deputy Emmett Slaughter's his name — but of course,
you know that already. And to his credit, Slaughter
revealed no information about you, not even when I
threatened his job. You didn't leave *much* of a trail — but
you left enough. Once I heard the Prewitt Gang were
looking so desperately for you, I was able to figure out
which way they'd go, and knew just where they'd end up."

"You're cracked, son," I told him, and I gripped his
shoulder — not hard like to hurt him, but friendly-like, as if
in sympathy of his mental state. "Listen up now, young

Deputy Golden. I don't know *why* that man on the ground's still asleep, but clearly, I barely winged him. Just took some flesh off, outside of his arm. You can see that yourself."

"Yes, but—"

"Proud of that shot I am, too — oh, I'm not bad close up, but I'd usually miss from that range. Hundred yards, maybe more, which is pretty fine shootin' I reckon! Now, that Frakes feller was rude and ungracious that one time I met him — but to give the man his due, he'd just shot a road agent clean through the eye, while riding a galloping horse. You *do* take my point, son?"

"He's got you there, Luke," said Rollins. "Every man west of Pittsburgh knows Lyle Frakes' reputation — he'd have killed this man here without doubt." Rollins was still sitting his horse, when he should have taken his weight off the animal's back after all that hard riding.

"Mister Frakes here is sixty years old," said Deputy Luke Golden then. And he wore a smile so smug, I wanted to wipe it right off of his face with my fists. *Then* he added, "Even the best of men loses his eyesight a little, and can't shoot so straight as he used to before he got old."

Old.

Old indeed.

But somehow, I *still* didn't hit him.

It was Marshal Rollins broke the silence. *"Are* you Lyle Frakes?" He didn't look too pleased about it. "If you are, you should have informed me, what with *me* being the Law here! And now you've brought trouble to our peaceful town, innocent folks could get *killed.*"

"Get down off that poor horse, you damn fool," I growled at him. "Take both them horses to the creek for a drink, 'fore I lose what remains of my temper."

"Mister Frakes, please," the smug Deputy went on. "How many men do you see, six feet tall weighing two-hundred pounds, wearing moccasins and—?"

"So every man my size wearing comfortable shoes must be him? Why, that explains *everything* now — there must be *hundreds* of Frakeses, no wonder folks think he's so good, he gets the credit for everything done between here and New York."

"There's only one Lyle Frakes," he replied, "and there's no doubt in my mind he's standing right here — even though he's shaved off his beard and gotten quite old."

Well, how much *can* one man take?

How much *should* a man take, more the point?

I lay Gertrude down on the grass, took two steps toward the arrogant young cuss, put my hands up and said, "Old am I then? Raise up your two fists and we'll see."

But instead of doing what was right, what was honorable and true, that damn young pup drew his six-gun — quick he was too, so quick my eyes barely seen it — and he said, "I *will* shoot you if I have to, Mister Frakes, sir."

"Damn you," I answered — for I saw by his eyes that he meant what he said — and so I stood by, let my fists fall down by my sides.

Oh, his time would come.

"If you'd only allowed me to finish, Mister Frakes, I was going to mention how *you* own a fine blue-eyed horse. A wonderful horse, not so famous as you are, but still, written up in newspapers from time to time this past dozen years. A powerful pale-faced stallion, so distinctive in looks and fine bearing, that he could not be missed by any man who knew what to look for."

"*Pale-Eye Champion Blaze*," said Town Marshal Rollins, his voice sounding powerfully shocked. "And to think how the townsfolk mocked the childish name of the horse when you first arrived."

"Mock my *Horse?* Why, you dirty sniveling..."

I must have looked murderous right about then, for the pear-shaped man scurried away, his expression alarmed — but he finally led their horses across to the dam, so at least it done *some* good.

Then Deputy Marshal Luke Golden nodded — a little to my left and behind me — to where Horse himself was now standing, inquisitive as ever. His eyes had never looked bluer than right in that moment, as he stretched his neck downways to sniff at the unconscious feller — probably deciding whether or not he should bite the skunk while he was down.

"Blue-eyed pale-faced traitor," I growled at Horse, who shoulda knowed to stay hidden when new men were about. "And to think, I coulda sold you two-hundred times — and every dang offer I got was for more than you're worth."

Without so much as one glance at that smug young pup Deputy, I turned away from him, kicked the unconscious man a well-deserved one in his ribs, and walked off to the creek to help Rollins rub down that pair of poor mistreated horses.

At least *they* wasn't traitors.

CHAPTER 4
BUSTED TEETH WEREN'T THE
WORST PART

I got Town Marshal Rollins started on rubbing them horses down proper, then told him I'd be a few minutes. "I'll go hitch up my wagon — help you cart the prisoner back into town. Better that, than you further mistreating your horse."

"You could just lend us one of your horses instead if—"

"After seein' how you treat your own?" I glanced across at Deputy Golden and the unconscious Prewitt feller, then turned back to Rollins. "Tell your *friend* I'll bring the wagon out in a few minutes."

Back in the house, I told Georgina And Mary the unconscious feller was alive — and they should get 'emselves ready for a quick trip to town.

"Ain't leaving you here unprotected," I said. "And I don't got no faith in these two useless lawmen, to take the man in without help."

Georgina gripped my arm and looked into my eyes — she could read me clear as words in a book, anytime I was troubled. "Oh, Kit," she said. "The Town Marshal knows who we are then? Must the townsfolk be told?"

"I'm sorry, Princess," I said — I had taken to calling her that on occasion, and I do believe she secretly liked it. "See, that skunk lying on the ground out there, he ain't gonna die — out cold, but mostly uninjured. Way the law works, there'll be a trial, and my real name will come out."

"No way around it then," said my beautiful silver-haired wife, and she cupped my cheek with her soft hand. "Don't worry, Kit, it'll be fine once people around here get used to it. They surely can't *blame* us for changing our names, especially not after this. They'll understand."

Little Mary's eyes shone with excitement — she always loved an adventure, and though the Princess disapproved, the child would make me tell her stories from my violent past whenever she could. Somehow though, Mary managed to keep her voice calm and even in front of Georgina. "It *is* the Prewitts, isn't it, Father?"

"I musta made a mistake," I said, roughing her hair. "Somehow they found out I was here. Don't worry, my lovelies, you know I can deal with this. But we'll have to take extra care from now on, even once I get rid of the Prewitts, for there's always *someone* out for revenge. Maybe we'll move somewhere else and start over."

"But my friends!"

"It's alright, Mary," said Georgina. "We won't be going *anywhere,* this is our home now. Trust your father, Mary, he can deal with *any* unpleasantness — he always has done so before."

A few minutes later, we three drove out from our barn

in the wagon. It's a heavy conveyance alright — thick planks high up both sides for protection from bullets, two planks high front and back too, so there's cover when you lie down inside it. That thing takes two horses to properly pull it, some of the steep hills we have around here — but I built it that way for a reason, and its time had arrived.

"You two keep quiet back there," I said, closing the curtain between me and my girls, who were lying down on a soft bed of comfortable straw. "I don't want these three skunks to know you're riding along. Our little secret. Good training for you both too, I reckon."

There was a *"HMMPH"* from Georgina, but I only smiled to myself, never let on I'd heard. I didn't figure the silence could last long — Georgina knew how to hobble her lips, but it'd be easier to teach Horse to shoot, than get little Mary to stay quiet for a half-hour.

Horse joined in, trailing behind us, way he usually does — I'd thrown his saddle and gear in the back of the wagon, just in case it was needed — and a half-minute later we approached the three men, who were waiting right about where I'd left them.

Town Marshal Samuel Rollins stood away from the others, holding onto the horses. At least *they* looked happier now.

As for Deputy Luke Golden, he was speaking with his prisoner. The murderous skunk was standing up on his hind legs now, but faced away from me.

Ain't much for size.

I'd have paid a dollar or three to hear what they were saying, but what with the clip-clop of my three horses' hooves and the rattling of boards and the rolling of wheels, I couldn't make out a word of it.

The shot feller's wound had been tended — Golden had torn the man's sleeve off and fashioned a dressing of sorts around the upper arm, a small spot of blood soaking through. It was clear the young man weren't much hurt.

Deputy Golden looked up as I pulled on the brake. "I appreciate your help, Mister Frakes. But to be clear, this man is *my* prisoner — if you kick him again, or any way otherwise hurt him, I *will* arrest you."

I hoped Georgina hadn't heard — she mostly disapproves of my less-than-delicate methods. I jumped down to the ground, and approached Deputy Luke Golden before quietly saying, "I'll do more than kick the skunk if he don't tell me where the rest of his brothers are hiding."

The shot feller tried not to look fearful, but he shrunk away from my gaze some. He hightailed it round behind Golden, like as if that could really protect him if I lost my temper. Thing was though, now I looked at him proper, he weren't even full growed — poor scared kid could not have been more than sixteen, I now noticed, him being not actually clean-shaved, but mildly fuzz-faced, the first beard of youth.

"He won't tell you a thing, Frakes," said Luke Golden, waving away the suggestion just like it meant nothing. "These Prewitts won't say a word once they're caught. Not after what happened the last time."

"Last time?"

"This man's not the first Prewitt I've captured," said

Golden, a hint too much pride in his voice. "They robbed a—"

"We should hit the trail," I said. "Get this feller locked away before the others come up with a plan to retrieve him. You can fill me in on what happened as we go along."

He didn't like me taking over, but knew I was right.

The young prisoner stayed wary of me — kept out of kicking range, would be my main meaning — as he walked toward the rear of the wagon.

"Nope," I said. "You'll sit beside me up front. Untie him, Deputy Golden, he can't be expected to sit on the box seat with his hands tied up 'hind his back."

Again, young Deputy Luke didn't like what I'd said, but he went along with it.

As he was being untied, the kid nodded an uncertain thanks, and I nodded back to him as I clambered up onto my box seat.

"Before you climb up though," I said, "I *will* hear your name. I won't hurt you none, or ask no other questions — but no man rides on my wagon 'less I know his name."

Strange thing, his gaze went from my eyes to Golden's, who nodded slightly before saying, "You heard him, prisoner. It's a long way to walk."

"I'm Squirrel," he said. "Squirrel Prewitt."

"You sure ain't," I growled at him. "I'll have the truth or you'll be dragged behind, up to you."

"But I am," he said, and he looked even younger right now, like as if he might cry.

"Prewitts don't have foolish names, son," I said. "They have simple names like Tom and Joe. Come to think, you ain't nearly ugly enough to be one a'them low snakes neither. You really a Prewitt or ain't you?"

His lip wobbled as he looked at me, and he sniffed before saying, "No questions, you promised, except for my name. It's the truth, my name's Squirrel Prewitt, I can't say nothing else."

"Fair enough then," said I. "Climb on up, and be sure to behave if you wish to keep breathing for long."

Rollins and Golden mounted their horses, and our journey proper commenced.

We went along silent the first bit, then Golden rode up beside me and went back to telling the story he'd started before — his voice still too prideful.

"Prewitt Gang robbed a payroll in Colorado Springs," he told me, "just on two months ago now. Another Deputy and I were in Denver then. We were assigned to the case, and we found them two nights after that — or rather, the Prewitts found us. Not knowing we were lawmen, they attempted to rob us, and received more than they'd bargained for."

"How many?"

"Hard to tell, Frakes, it was too dark. But we believe there were eight at that time. There was a gunfight, one of their number was injured, and another was trapped underneath her horse when it fell. I arrested them both, took them in."

"*Her* horse, you say?" I took a tighter hold on my horses as we commenced the steep descent into the canyon, before saying, "So one of their gang is a woman? Reckon I woulda noticed if one a'them six today was a filly. So I guess she's in jail now then?"

"No. That's not how it went."

"Best I shut up," I said, "and just let you finish."

"My partner died from his wounds not long after we made it to town, so I charged them with murder. The woman refused to say anything — told us Prewitts don't sing."

"And the man?"

"Oh, Jimmy Prewitt sang loud — he informed on the others in exchange for a lenient sentence. But two nights before the trial was scheduled, the Deputy guarding the jailhouse had his throat cut. By the time he was found in the morning, Eliza Prewitt was long gone."

I tried to read Luke Golden's eyes, but there weren't nothing in them to read, so I asked him, "And Jimmy himself?"

"Well, they left four of his fingers on the desk in the jailhouse — arranged them so they resembled a wide open mouth."

"How could you be sure it was a mouth? Mighta been—"

"Oh, it was a mouth alright," Golden said. "Most of Jimmy Prewitt's teeth were arranged in two rows inside the mouth, still bloody and broken. A terrible sight, I assure you. Fingers and teeth, what a thing."

I turned to look at young Squirrel, but he turned away. I looked back at Luke Golden and said, "But they took this Jimmy along with them anyway?"

"Not far. They cut off what was left of Jimmy's hand and nailed it to the signpost at the south end of town — its one remaining finger pointing up into a tree. And when you looked where the finger was pointed..."

He paused for effect, way young fellers do, but I didn't say a word, only waited until he went on.

"...They had hung their own brother from the tree, not by his neck, but instead by his ... they hung him up by his privates, Mister Frakes, after cutting and slicing him some."

"Dead then."

"Very much so when he was found. But it would have been slow and painful. Young Squirrel won't tell us a thing — I can guarantee that."

CHAPTER 5
AN EASY TARGET

As we entered the streets of Santa Monica proper, I was thinking 'bout what might soon happen, what with young Squirrel Prewitt about to be locked in the jailhouse.

Worried me some, was the truth. With Santa Monica being a town of under four-hundred souls — all more-or-less law-abiding folk — Rollins was the town's only lawman.

Sure, I was no friend to the Marshal, and indeed, thought little of the man — but he *did* have a family to consider. Put simple, I had no wish to see his children orphaned at such a young age. Poor tykes had lost their mother already — and while Rollins's own mother was a help to him, she could not be expected to raise her grandchildren alone.

Rollins would be an easy target for such as the Prewitts. Any gang who could bust their members out of a *proper* jailhouse like Colorado Springs, would make short work of a pen-pusher like Samuel Rollins.

We trundled along Utah Street, past the neat rows of well-painted houses with their new picket fences and gardens, and finally came to where the shops all stood waiting for business, both sides of Third Street. Not a *busy* town exactly, but especially here in the middle part, Santa Monica had a real pleasant bustle to it. I guess it was its clever-worded signs and extra-wide streets, and all them top-quality windows, all cleaned within an inch a'their lives at least once a day, made the place sorta shine.

And as for the neat well-dressed people who strode all about, they seemed more genteel somehow than most Western townsfolk — at least if you went by their looks and the state of their grooming.

But for all these folks' fancy manners, their beaks weren't no less sticky than the ordinary folks I have known in other places.

Towns is towns, and gossips is gossips — and wherever you find the first, there'll be plenty of the second to spread out the news good'n'timely.

And right now, there was heads turning round on their necks, and mouths running fifteen to the dozen, as folks stepped out of shops to see just *who* these newcomers were — namely Squirrel and Golden. I nodded a howdy to a few folks I knew, and tried to ignore all the others.

Always best to keep to yourself, add no fuel to the fire of town gossip, if you can help it.

I whistled and motioned for Deputy Luke Golden to

drop back alongside me again. He scanned the street ahead before doing so, just like he should have.

"You plan to sleep in the jailhouse, Golden?" I asked quietly as he came alongside. "Damn Prewitts'll cut Rollins in slices if you ain't there to help guard your prisoner."

"I need to go after the rest of the Prewitts," he answered. "Perhaps *you* could help guard the—"

"Got my own family to protect, if you ain't noticed. I reckon you'd do best to set up an ambush — you know these Prewitts will come for this feller, just as they done it last time."

"I don't believe they will," Golden said, his smile smug once again, as he looked across at young Squirrel, and nodded toward him. "I doubt this one's much valued by them."

"By what reckoning?"

"You have a big reputation, Frakes, yet you seem to miss obvious things." *More damn smug than ever.* "For a first thing, the way they sent him ahead to be shot at first — did you really not notice that, Frakes? And also, they rode away soon as you shot him, just left him for dead."

"You seen all that from back where you was, did you, Golden?"

"Young eyes, sir," he said, and *winked* at me. "And besides, they most probably think the kid's dead. They'd have seen how he never moved after he hit the ground."

"Well, if you know so much ... *Deputy* ... you'll *know* you can't leave him here for Sam Rollins to protect — he ain't up to the job if they come for the kid, and there ain't nothin' else to it. Gross negligence it'll be called, and you'll lose your job, rightly so, or my name ain't Kit..."

It was gonna take some getting used to again — I had been Kit Farmer a year now.

At least *someone* was amused by my plight.

"Lyle Frakes, I believe you *meant* to say," said the smug-faced pup with a laugh. "Or are you *truly* Kit Farmer now, having lost all the skills you were known for when you were Frakes? Either way, sir, you're right about one thing, this town picked a dud — Marshal Rollins is useless."

"He ain't entirely—"

"We'd best head to Los Angeles then," Golden said, "unless you want Rollins's death on your conscience. The prisoner will have to go there for his trial anyway, so we *could* just take him there now. I'll leave that up to *you* to decide, Mister Frakes."

"Oh yes please," came little Mary's voice from beside me, and I quickly turned to see her head had popped through the curtain between me and young Squirrel. "Oh please, Father, can't we, we've not been for so long, and it'll be *such* an adventure to travel with this mean outlaw Squirrel Prewitt, and what an odd name, and oh, you're really quite handsome for such a mean fellow, I thought you'd be an ugly brute, but I've been almost *dying* to sneak a look at you, and oh my lord look at the *Deputy,* he's even *more* handsome, oh Mother, you simply *must* see how handsome this—"

"Mary Farmer, you stop that this instant," cried Georgina, popping her head out to glare at our smiling daughter. "You must *never* speak that way of men, not in

front of them anyway. Now leave your father to deal with ... oh dear, yes, I see *quite* what you mean, he is *unusually* handsome, my goodness."

I pulled the brake hard — had to put out a hand to grab Mary, as she almost went tumbling over the box seat and onto the street.

"I'm sorry, Kit," said Georgina. "She did well to keep quiet so long, don't you think? You should probably introduce us to your new friend, now he knows that we're here."

His horse reared a little — Golden's way of playing to the gallery, I believe, for it was done stylish-like, with no loss of control — then the animal wheeled about in a perfect half circle, stopping so the man himself was right up close beside me, still wearing that smile.

I turned away from him, not acknowledging the trick. "He ain't no friend a'mine," I growled at Georgina, "and there ain't no use in you getting to know him. Soon as he gets this feller locked up, he'll be going off to get killed by the rest a'the Prewitts. So both you girls get in the back there, where you was told to."

"Oh, that's a *terrible* shame, Mother, isn't it?" chirped little Mary. "We simply *must* invite the brave lawman to dinner, for we cannot allow him to be killed without a nice meal to warm his—"

"Now you stop that, Mary," I growled. "This pup ain't welcome on my place, you both get in the back and forget about—"

"You *must* forgive my husband's manners," Georgina said, leaning across me to offer her hand to that smug skunk

Golden to shake. "The events of today have been quite a shock, and he's not his usual self. I'm Georgina, and our daughter is Mary."

"Charmed to meet two such lovely ladies," the Deputy said, putting on his best smooth-faced smile. And he not only took my wife's hand in his own filthy paw, the damn snake bent down and he *kissed* it.

Well, if he wished to be punched in the face, he shoulda just said so.

CHAPTER 6
ELBOWS & KNEES, PUNCHES & GOUGES

Sometimes you don't stop to think, you just act.

Bad enough the young skunk touched Georgina's hand, but when he put his filthy lips on her, I launched myself at him, and knocked the loose-lipped *Lothario* clean from his horse.

I got one good punch in as we flew through the air, and a second as we hit the ground — me on top of him, with the advantage.

He roared and he squealed and he bucked, but even with youth on his side, young Golden weren't much of a scrapper. Not that I gave him much chance to get a punch in — older man has to take his opportunities, I reckon, so I was all elbows and knees and punches and gouges. Head-butted him once or twice too — my head being hard and not much use for anything else.

I half-heard the noises around us — some of it cheers, some chastisements — as a crowd gathered round, way they do when a rare entertainment starts up.

But it's funny, how through all them noises, the only voices you properly hear are those of your loved ones.

"Kit, *stop it,* you're killing the man," cried Georgina, as I smashed a well-aimed right fist against Golden's jaw.

And as I drew back my elbow, crashed it against the other side of his face, I heard Mary call, "Stop, Father, please, I can't marry the man if you *kill* him."

I don't know quite *why* their words stopped me. But all violence left me right then, seeped out of me, all drained away, like as if something in me had died.

I looked down into Deputy Luke Golden's face — all covered in blood and saliva and snot, his left eye already swelling, his right showing fear — and I wondered if there must be something wrong in my head, to have done such a thing.

He's a lawman, I thought. *Not an outlaw!* And it horrified me some, what I'd done, verifiably shook me.

That's when I heard an unmistakeable click — the hammer of a big six-gun behind me, not a yard away from my head.

"Enough, Mister Farmer — I mean *Frakes,*" said Marshal Sam Rollins. "You're in enough trouble already, without killing a Federal Deputy. Step away from him, please, and raise your hands in the air."

I raised my hands up right away, moved nice and slow, but stayed where I was — and I looked across at my girls, who had climbed from the wagon down onto the street. They were huddled together, staring at me like I was a stranger. And right then I felt older and tireder than a still-breathing body has a right to. Felt old as a rock, but maybe not nearly so clever.

"Don't shoot him, please, Marshal Rollins," said Georgina. "He's still the same man you've known."

"Course I won't shoot, not unless I have to," came Rollins's voice from behind me. "Please, Mister Frakes, climb off the man now, you've done enough damage for one day."

"I'm sorry," I said quietly to Golden. "Might be I got carried away some."

I climbed off of him then. Took every last ounce of strength in my body to push myself to my feet, and walk the half-dozen steps across to lean against my own wagon.

Musta been twenty-five people all gathered around, they had poured on out from the hardware store and the haberdashery and the bakery too, and it seemed to me like they all started talking right then — I've no idea what they said, and I didn't care.

Thing was though, some of those folks were women and children, which made me more ashamed what I'd done.

There weren't one friendly face in the whole town I reckon — not friendly to *me* anyway. Georgina and Mary were attending to Luke Golden now, and even Horse just shook his head at me, stamped his front foot on the ground, and said something in horse-talk that mighta been a bad cuss-word.

By the time Golden got helped to his feet, and was getting his face cleaned of blood by my wife, I started to notice a few things the townsfolk was saying.

The words "Lyle Frakes" seemed to be spreading like wildfire, and all hope of continuing my quiet life as Kit Farmer seemed all burned away. Whole lotta tut-tutting from them townsfolk too, when it started to get around that Luke Golden was a U.S. Deputy Marshal.

"All you people move on now," Rollins called at the top of his voice, as he waved his gun at them. "There's nothing more here to see, go back to your business and let us alone."

Strangest thing in all this was the actions of young Squirrel Prewitt — in all a'that ruckus, he had been left alone, all forgotten.

If you'll recall, he was untied, and also barely injured aside from a flesh wound to one of his arms.

Not just that, but I had made a *damn* foolish mistake. I had left Squirrel unwatched on my wagon with Gertrude — *Gertrude, my beautiful rifle, all loaded and ready for trouble* — and yet, young Squirrel had not moved from his seat; had not tried to escape; had not armed himself; and indeed, had not done *anything* I'd have expected from an unguarded prisoner.

It worried me, that fool mistake — showed my skills and instincts was rusty, and it didn't bode well.

I made my way to Squirrel now, said, "Why the hell are you still here, young feller? You coulda took up my gun, or at least run away, you woulda been long gone by now."

He looked sorta puzzled, then half-smiled at me as he rubbed at the fuzz on his chin. "Never thought a'that, Mister Frakes. I just do what I'm told most the time, and the fact is, no one said *Run*."

Not sure why I found it so funny, but it tickled me

some, and the laughter burst right on outta me, I couldn't stop it.

Well, I reckon the kid seen the funny side too, and we musta made for a sight, us pair of undesirables laughin' together — didn't impress Georgina, that much I do know. If eyes could scrape skin off a man, there'd be nothin' of me left but bone. Perhaps not even that.

"Maybe I am gettin' old after all, young Squirrel," I said to the kid. "Gettin' friendly with you after you tried to kill me — yet taking my fists to the lawman who came here to save me. Ain't right behavior now, is it? I must be gone in the brain."

Squirrel Prewitt stopped his laughing right then, looked at me real serious. Then he blinked hard a couple a'times, like his head hurt or something. "Weren't nothin' personal, Mister Frakes," the kid said, "and I reckon I'm terrible sorry. Like I said, I just do what I'm told."

There was something about him I liked, an honesty maybe, someplace inside where it mattered. He didn't look like no outlaw, and didn't sound like one neither. He was just some poor kid who'd been caught up in a bad family.

I felt somehow *fatherly* toward him I guess.

Rollins and Golden and my two girls was headed our way now — none of 'em looked too happy with me — so in our last moments alone, I offered the kid some advice.

"When you get outta jail, you go straight, young Squirrel, you hear me? Don't listen to the rest a'them Prewitts no more, keep away from 'em, do your own thinking. It ain't too late for you, Squirrel, you're young and your character ain't hardened up yet — you might yet become a good man, that's all I'm saying. And it's *your* choice to make."

CHAPTER 7

"IF YOU'RE DONE WITH SHOOTING YOUR MOUTH OFF..."

When a man finds himself in the dog house and knows he deserves it, he finds himself agreeing to things he normally wouldn't.

Don't get me wrong — I was always going to help take young Squirrel to Los Angeles. The Prewitts *had* come here to kill *me,* and I could not allow Samuel Rollins to be murdered while guarding him.

But when Georgina ordered me to throw my saddle on Horse, because *"Deputy Luke is in no fit condition to ride,"* well, I bit my lip hard enough to draw blood, and I managed not to say what I thought.

Sure, Golden's left eye was half-closed, he had a cut under the other, and his lip was split some. And okay, one of his teeth had worked loose, but it ain't like I'd broke it off jagged.

His fine handsome nose wasn't busted — nor his limbs or his skull — and him being a U.S. Deputy Marshal, he shoulda been able to ride how he was, no complaints, no delays.

When I worked that same job right after the war, we was often busted and broken, and it never stopped *us*.

But anyway, that's how we traveled to Los Angeles — Georgina and Mary in back of the wagon; Squirrel sitting up front where he'd been all along; and Luke dang Golden's rear end parked on *my* seat.

Rollins rode in front, I rode behind, and it was an unpleasant trip — for me anyway. Not for my girls or for Golden, they all chatted away like old friends, ignored me the whole time.

What we *should* have done was go on the train — but a month ago, little ways south, a prisoner tried to escape while being brought in by a wet-behind-the-ears Deputy, and the train's guard got himself killed by trying to help. The rail company jumped up and down and called a meeting in Los Angeles — upshot was that prisoners can no longer be taken on trains without a permit signed by the County Sheriff, the Mayor, and some bigwig from the railroad company itself.

Like as if enforcing the laws ain't hard enough already, you now need your paperwork done in advance, before a crime's been committed. Whole dang world's going mad, all tied up in red tape, and just keeps gettin' more foolish.

Well, they can keep their dang iron horses anyway, I prefer flesh and blood ones.

It was just about late afternoon when we pulled up out front of the County Sheriff's Office in Los Angeles.

Sheriff Sullivan Simms himself was on duty — on duty,

not actually working, way I reckon things. Man of leisure, if ever there was one. He was rocking himself in a chair on the porch, a cloud of white smoke all around him, as he puffed on a big fat cigar.

I have never quite understood smoking — plain fact is, it's an unpleasant odor, and it's only the smoker himself who ever says otherwise. Just my opinion, for what it's worth anyway, which is a'course less than two pennies. Then again, maybe some folks have a good use for foul breath — just don't get me started on them that chews their tobacco.

And Simms was a man who did both.

"Why, it's Deputy Marshal Luke Golden," said the Sheriff — overly friendly he seemed — while continuing to rock in his chair. "That there one a'them Prewitts you been hunting, son?"

"One down, six to go, Sheriff," said Golden, stepping down to the street.

I noted, with some satisfaction, his shiner was now a bright purple, the eye three-parts closed from the swelling.

"You sure he's a Prewitt?" said Sheriff Simms as he studied young Squirrel. "Looks like only a kid, I thought they was all older. He ever killed anyone yet?"

Town Marshal Rollins had seemed keen to get noticed by the big-city Sheriff, and grasped his opportunity now. He wheeled his horse about, close up by the porch rail and said, "Not that we know of, Sheriff Simms."

That slippery cigar-smokin' Simms looked now at the Santa Monica Marshal — looked at him like he was something sticky and stinky he'd found on the bottom of his boot. "Do not speak unless spoken to, Rollins — this whole County is *my* jurisdiction, including your quiet corner of it."

"I was only trying to—"

"You'd only get in the way, *Town* Marshal Rollins. There's *real* lawmen doing *real* law work here. Perhaps you hadn't noticed, but *this* is a dangerous and serious business. You should have stayed in your quiet little town, where your meagre talents are suited. Frankly, I've no idea *why* they even employ you."

I felt bad for Rollins, so I did not look at him. I looked at Luke Golden instead.

Golden smiled that smug smile he favored, shrugged his shoulders at Rollins, and thereafter ignored him completely. He wiggled his finger for Squirrel to climb down from the box seat, and the prisoner did so without hesitation. Then Golden turned to Sheriff Simms and explained, "As a member of the Prewitt gang, it's very likely Squirrel Prewitt has been with them when they've killed men."

"But perhaps not killed any himself?"

"That will be for Judge Adams to decide when the prisoner stands trial," said Golden, taking Squirrel's undamaged arm and marching him up the steps onto the porch. "For now, he's charged only with *attempted* murder. He tried to kill Lyle Frakes here, and was injured in the process when Frakes shot him off of his horse."

Sheriff Simms gave no indication of surprise upon hearing my name, and continued to ignore me. He looked only at the prisoner and said, "Young skunk looks healthy to me. Sure he didn't just *fall* off the horse? Won't bother bringing the Doc for the useless young fool."

"It's a flesh wound, I already cleaned it," said Golden, grabbing Squirrel's arm to spin him around so the lazy, still-seated Sheriff could see where the blood had soaked through the dressing. "The prisoner was lucky, I guess. Mister Frakes must be rusty, or perhaps his eyes have got old. Either way though, the prisoner has rights, and therefore *must* be seen by a doctor if one is available."

"He's not the only one here needs a doctor," Simms exclaimed, having finally noticed the condition of Luke Golden's face. Simms whistled through his teeth and he added, "What the hell happened, young Luke? Prisoner bash you with a shovel when you tried to arrest him? You look like you just fought a bear."

"Mister Frakes and I had a slight misunderstanding," said Golden, and he looked outright mirthful, considering how beaten up he was. "It's all sorted now, Sheriff Simms, I assure you. Frakes even offered me the use of his wagon, and rode along to protect me while I brought in the prisoner, as you can see."

I had only once briefly met Sheriff Sullivan Simms, that being when he notarized the deed to our land. He was baldy and scarred some near his left ear, and was aged perhaps forty-five — looked like a man who had lived a hard life, but been tough enough to survive it, and had therefore earned some respect.

Although, the way he'd treated Rollins, I'd took a few points off already. Still, Simms had been a lawman for years, with a tough reputation, so he still had points in the bank.

He stood up from his seat now, first looking down his nose at Horse, then the same way at me. When he spoke, he made his voice deeper than it sounded before. "So you really *are* the famed Lyle Frakes."

"Don't know about famed, but I'm Frakes."

"Well, I'll tell you something for free, Frakes. Your reputation was built long ago, and may or may *not* have been earned — but to *me,* you're just another old man with no respect for the law."

"That ain't nohow true, Sheriff—"

"You shut your mouth now Frakes and listen to ME!"

He had yelled it, when he'd have been better off to say the words quiet and menacing. Consequently, my opinion of Sullivan Simms went down one more notch — but I did what he said, he *is* the law here after all. So I made a great show of shutting my mouth, smiled at him with my whole face, and cupped my right ear with my hand — showing how much I *respected* him, you understand.

He sure did glare at me then, Sheriff Sullivan Simms did. Went the color of Red Mountain at sunset, and the spittle flew from his mouth when he started up speaking again. "You *lied* to me when you arrived, Frakes — gave *me* a false name. And *now* you've made a vicious attack on a lawman, a U.S. Deputy Marshal who's here to protect you. You'll do three nights here in the cells, just for starters — the Judge went to San Francisco for a funeral, and won't be back until Tuesday."

That's it, I decided. *Time to use an old trick, angrify him by constantly using his full name and title — undermines a skunk some with no extra effort, would be why you might choose to do so. Try it sometime, you'll enjoy it.*

"You must got some wax in your ears, Sheriff Sullivan Simms," I said calmly, and Horse shifted under me some, way he does when he senses there might soon be a frolic[1]. "It was simply a misunderstanding, he ain't pressing no charges. Right, Golden?"

"That's quite true, Sheriff Simms," said the Deputy. He actually winked at me then — with his good eye, a'course, not the one almost closed — before turning back toward Simms. "Indeed, the whole Frakes family and I are on friendly terms now. So much so that his *lovely* wife and daughter — that's the two pretty ladies who just climbed out of the wagon there — have invited me for a meal at their family home."

I did not say a word, did not flinch, did not look at Georgina.

Simms touched the brim of his hat, gave a grudging nod to my girls, then looked back at me and Horse. "Well, that's a pity," he said. "However, there's more to *this* than assault. You lied to *me,* Frakes. I'm the Law around here, and you gave *me* a false name when you bought your land. There's laws about hiding your identity from a lawman who—"

"Which law would that be, *Sheriff* Sullivan Simms? Do you *know* the laws? Because *I* surely do. And as an ex-lawman, I have the right to use a false name, if using my own might endanger myself or my family — but maybe you knew that already. Reckon it's time you stopped this harassment and done somethin' useful, like take charge of the prisoner the Deputy brung you — and once you're done with that, you might wish to read one a'them law books you got in this big fancy building, brush up some on your knowledge. That is, if you're all done with sitting and smoking and shooting your mouth off."

"You can't speak to *me* that way you—"

"Or you could stop hiding in town here, team up with Golden, go after them Prewitts — they're in *your* jurisdiction, after all. Or are you afraid of *real* law work, *Sheriff* Sullivan Simms?"

---

1. FROLIC: For most folks, this means a party, a celebration, or a wild time. But in the West, it more often means a fight, with fists or with guns, or anything else comes to hand. Like I said, a party or wild time...

CHAPTER 8

THE PRICE OF MARITAL PEACE

I t being late afternoon, I figured it'd be safer to stay the night at a hotel, and head back home in the morning. Too many places for ambush, to travel at night with Prewitts around.

An added benefit to this, was that it might go a ways toward getting me out of the dog house. Georgina and Mary both love to go poking through stores that sell dresses and hats and perfumes and such — even seems like their satisfaction doubles when those stores are expensive, like the fancier ones in Los Angeles.

It seemed strange the way Luke Golden backed me when Sheriff Simms wanted to jail me. Perhaps Golden felt bad about what he'd done, understood he was wrong to push me so far.

Either way, I sure wasn't sorry for anything I'd said to Sullivan Simms. He was an experienced Sheriff, and shoulda knowed better at his age — and it weren't only me he'd disrespected, he'd talked down at Sam Rollins in front of us all. Weren't right to do so, even though he *was* mostly correct about Rollins being useless.

You just don't belittle a fellow lawman that way, not in front of others.

Once they took the prisoner inside, I announced we'd be doing some shopping then staying the night — got a smile from Mary, but no sugar at all from my wife.

Then I warned our Town Marshal not to try tracking them Prewitts by himself — told him that even *I* was not stupid enough to try it alone, and that it would take a whole team of men working together to take the gang in.

"Well, when you put it like that," Rollins answered — and he sounded relieved — "I guess I'll get the train home, make my usual patrols of the town, and not go out looking for Prewitts."

We said our goodbyes to him then, and my true difficulties began — those related to shopping.

Like a dutiful husband and father, I accompanied Georgina and Mary while they spent too much of our money on frivolous things. First store we went into was some sorta fancy perfumery. It verifiably reeked of lotions and potions that woulda killed a horse if it had the bad luck to wander in through them huge doors — ten feet high them dang doors were, which sorta impressed me. But it all went downhill from there.

Flummoxed[1] my sniffer that place did — problem was, it smelled like a big-city cathouse, the sort that costs triple what most do. I kept expectin' to see whole rows of ladies wearin' nothin' but frillies, and kickin' their feet up so high you might lose an eye if you didn't look elsewhere.

Not that I'd know that such places exist — I'm just sayin', I heard tell that they might.

Anyway, seemed to me like that stinkin' perfumery had been specially selected by my wife to maximize my suffering — and it didn't end there.

From there we crossed the street and entered a store that might be best described as *The Bottomless Pit of Fool Fashions* — well, I *almost* said what I thought, but managed to catch it in time. Clamped my mouth tight shut then, and only let it open when asked my opinion of a dress or a hat or some fool pair of twelve-dollar shoes. Then I waxed somewhat lyrical on how pretty the thing was — *although not so pretty as the one who was tryin' it on* — and insisted on buying it for them.

Another half-hour in, and I was suffering bad. I even felt sorry for the Prewitts — they would surely be disappointed, having come all this way to kill me, only to find that I'd died of more painful causes — *boredom by shopping,* I reckon it's probably called.

As I stood loyally by, managing a sorta smile every time Mary or Georgina held up some sorta sewing fabric or the like — this was the third store we'd been in — I believe I finally sighed, a pitiful noise that I felt rightly ashamed of. But lucky for me, my dear little Mary has ever been quick to forgive. Doesn't like to see animals suffer, I reckon, and she brightly suggested I might go to a saloon, or wait for them outside, as they'd be here an hour at least, and I was gettin' in the way.

Well, I could not hand over my roll of cash quick

enough, and hightailed it outta that place in about fourteen seconds flat.

If I was a sociable man, I mighta gone to the saloon, my nerves being worn down and frazzled by the shopping as they were. But with Prewitts about, I weren't goin' nowhere, so I waited outside a'the store.

I sure wasn't lonely outside there. There was three other fellers all waiting, and we stood about lookin' at each other and watching the looks on other suffering husbands when they got dragged in through the doors.

"What did you do to get brung along?" I asked one.

"Not sure," he answered, and he looked kinda puzzled. "It was right after I told her she was pretty as a horse. She just looked at me mean-like, all sudden, and tells me we's goin' out shoppin' for hats. She's got a lot more hats than heads, that much I do know."

"Strange cattle, women," I answered. "What did you do to get sent outside?"

"Strange that was too," he said then. "All I done was pass wind, and it was perfectly silent. She just tells me, 'Outside,' and I went."

"That's worth a try," I said, "if this ever happens to me again."

The other two fellers nodded agreement, and we passed the time quietly thereafter.

The shopping trip must have helped some I reckon, for by the time they were done it seemed I'd been mostly forgiven for beating on Golden — not *forgiven* exactly, but no more harsh words were said, even after Mary climbed into her bed in our fancy hotel room.

Twelve dang dollars for the night, that one room, can you believe it? I've seen men jailed a year for lesser robbery than that.

Next morning, Georgina still didn't have much to say to me. But before we went down to breakfast, Mary said she had a small gift for us. Told us we had to share it, then made us close our eyes before handing us a corner of it each.

"Alright, you can look now," she said.

It was a shiny white handkerchief she had bought the previous day — *no change from a dollar, I bet* — and in large looping red stitches she had embroidered a K and a P near the middle, with a heart right there in between them.

She smiled that beautiful smile a'hers and said, "The K is for Kit, of course, and the P for Princess. I was going to do L and G, but I like when you use the pet names you have for each other."

Then she hugged us both at the same time.

Well, I thanked the child and wiped some dirt outta my eye, and Georgina gave me a smile too. Not a big one, but something. And she scooped Mary up in her arms, and tickled the child until she was all outta breath.

I sure do love 'em both.

We ate a leisurely breakfast before leaving Los Angeles behind us. It was a big heavy breakfast I had inside me when we left, but I reckon I weighed about the same as when I rode into town — the difference made up by my wallet being two-hundred dollars lighter than it was yesterday.

A cheap price to pay for some marital peace. Still ... two-

hundred dang dollars. I reckon I might keep my fists to myself from now on.

We decided to attend the midday church service in Santa Monica on our way home. I had briefly argued against our attending, knowing how quick gossip spreads in a town of four-hundred. But Georgina felt it was important to treat the day just like any other Sunday — to show people that we were still the same family as before, just with the name Frakes instead of Farmer.

I suggested a vote, way I do when I don't get my way — and Mary sided with her mother, way she does just about every time. So of course, we'd be going to church, just like usual.

What weren't quite so usual was our journey — just about every half-hour, we heard shots fired.

Three shots each time — and from three different rifles.

These rifle shots was always behind us; always the same rhythm too.

One shot by itself, then a pause of five seconds, then two shots almost together.

Bang ... then a pause ... then bang-bang.

First time we heard it, I thought nothing much of it.

About a half-mile behind us, I thought. *Eight-hundred yards, give or take. Most likely folks hunting together.*

Second time though, a half-hour later, it bothered me how the rhythm of the shots was repeated. I didn't say nothing about it to Georgina and Mary.

Six-hundred yards, thereabouts.

Third time, I knew who it was — it had been a half-hour again. Same three shots; same three rifles; same exact rhythm.

Five-hundred yards.

Prewitts, playing a foolish dang game, hoping to rattle me some.

Well, they'll find out soon enough, I don't rattle easy. And when it comes time to play, I'll be up for the frolic.

---

1. FLUMMOXED: Confused or perplexed. (Like JV is every morning til he's had his coffee)

CHAPTER 9
ONE LUCKY MAN

I still didn't say anything about them rifle shots to my girls — but I kept an ear out the rest of the way as I drove.

Still, I wasn't too worried.

Horse wasn't tied to the wagon, and that animal's good as a watchdog. If anyone got within range of us, he'd sure let me know.

There was no further unwelcome noises the rest of the trip. But when we arrived at the church a half-hour early, it seemed like half of the Santa Monica townsfolk were already there — and they were pouring out of the Town Hall building next door.

Not just that, but it seemed like they mostly was gossiping — and by the way they all turned and pointed as we arrived, *we* was the subject of their gossip. Or maybe just *I* was, I guess — me being the bad-behaved citizen who'd beat up a visiting lawman the previous day.

Seemed like their mutual hatred of me was enough to

get the members of *all three* churches together on the Sabbath. Surprising what a good dose of mutual hatred can accomplish — even with good Christian folks. Weren't my proudest achievement.

Shoulda beat young Luke Golden up in someplace more private, I guess, instead of in town — small town news travels faster'n fire here in the West.

Still, there was something unusual about Santa Monica then — it was *not* your typical Western town.

To explain short and simple, it had no saloon whatsoever — and yet, like I said, three churches. Has to be *some* sorta record.

Anyway, the churches was all clustered around the Town Hall — and them churches was the center of things in Santa Monica, the be all and end all for most folks. Well, there was also the nice sandy beach, where some folks would just sit around when they had nothin' useful to do.

Most of the locals had paid quite big money for uselessly small blocks of land — five-hundred dollars the cheapest — when the town blocks went on sale, only three years ago, overlooking the ocean.

It was one of the things that attracted me to the place — no saloon would mean mostly no rough types, and less chance of me being recognized by men from my past. Sure, I had shaved off my beard, and no longer wore my preferred buckskin clothing — still wore my moccasins, a'course, some things can't be changed no matter what. But some folks look right into your eyes, recognize you by seeing inside you, if that makes any sense — and to start a quiet new life, I needed for *no one* to guess who I was.

It had worked out well for us too, Santa Monica. Like anywhere else, there was folks from most walks of life — but mostly the quieter, well-behaved types of people. Lots of young families, but plenty of older folk too, who had been told to live by the ocean for the good of their health — same reason me and Horse first got told we should come here. Good for old bones, in our case.

The weather was pleasant all year, the sea air invigorating, and even the heavy morning mists were agreeable somehow. And every time the mist cleared, the view of that endless ocean made me feel a sort of a *longing* — I don't know what *for* exactly — but it's a nice sorta longing, if that makes any sense.

Don't get me wrong, I love the land. The forests and mountains and critters and rocks, the beautiful rivers and streams of the West, have made my every day a pleasure this past sixty years — but the ocean is something extra to add to its beauty.

I am one lucky man.

I never much wondered what other folks thought of us when we first came. Looking back, I guess some mighta wondered how we had enough money to buy where we did, but no one ever pushed us to tell 'em. Our place was a few miles from town, the best I could find — Mary gasped when she first seen it, said it was *'just like a storybook,'* and asked if we could build a castle on the edge of the cliff, overlooking the waves and the sand down below.

And Georgina? She just smiled in a way that said *This is the place.*

We built a sensible ways back from the edge — not a

castle but a solid, strong, simple ranch house of logs and adobe. Still, it was some place alright — bordered by ocean, a canyon and a mountain, only one easy way in and out. And a stream running through for fresh water, and lots of good pasture.

Truth is, it took most of Georgina's money to buy it, then a fair chunk of mine to build the place up how we wanted.

Well, when we first came everyone was too polite to ask questions about us — but we were about to find out, such politeness was over.

As we got near the church, it was Marshal Sam Rollins who greeted us, and he seemed almost overly friendly.

"Mister Frakes," he said plenty loud as I pulled on the brake. "I'm glad you could make it, after yesterday's little unpleasantness. And Mrs Frakes, you look well. And good morning to you too, Miss Mary."

"Marshal," I replied with a nod. "No sign a'them Prewitts about?"

"None at all."

"I didn't get a proper chance to thank you yesterday, Marshal Rollins. You stood up when it mattered. I thank you for that."

He nodded and smiled, helped Georgina and Mary down from the wagon. Then under his breath, he said, "There's been a town meeting, some folks aren't too happy, finding out this way who you are. Might take time for some folks to adjust."

I tried to set my face to a fake smile — way his was —

and asked the man a straight question. "You a instigatory part a'that, Rollins?"

"I didn't call the meeting, if that's what you're asking. Indeed, they did not invite me. But when I realized there was a meeting, I went in and listened — that's part of my job, Mister Frakes, as you know." He waited a moment or two to let that sink in before going on. "Listen, I've had time to think now, and I understand, you did what you had to. But if anyone says something foolish — well, I hope you'll show some restraint. Please, Mister Frakes. Don't beat anyone else up, we all have to live here."

I studied him a moment, saw Rollins was doing his best in a difficult circumstance. I understood, too, that there *would* most likely be trouble — and decided I'd best restrict Horse from moving. That animal likes standing by and watching *two* men fight — just like anyone else does — but when there's a brawl that involves extra people, it takes him back to his days as a warhorse, and he has a bad habit of getting involved.

"Alright, Marshal," I finally agreed, as I finished tying Horse to the back of my wagon. "I'll keep my fists to myself while in town, unless someone hits me first. But let's keep an eye out for Prewitts. We ain't heard the last a'them boys, young Samuel Rollins. We best make sure to stay on our toes — this'll get worse before it gets better."

CHAPTER 10

VERMIN

W e was in for a difficult couple of days. As if killers weren't enough trouble, there was neighborly unrest to deal with too. When I was a single man, I would not have cared — but when someone upsets my family I feel it harshly, their pain being mine now to share.

First off, half our usual churchgoers went straight home without attending the service — including all three families Georgina and Mary were most friendly with.

Never even spoke to us, just hightailed it home, soon as they seen us arrive.

Georgina held her head high, way she always does when she's tested, and took Mary inside the church to wait, while I stayed and spoke with the Marshal. He told me Luke Golden had come by that morning, and delivered him a summons to serve me — I would have to attend the courthouse in Los Angeles Tuesday, as a witness in Squirrel Prewitt's trial.

Things didn't get no better once we all went inside, for it was a mighty strange sermon. The Town Preacher went on and on about wolves in sheep's clothing and such — at first I took that as a statement on men like the Prewitts. But when he mixed in some verses about farmers — meaning Kit and Georgina and Mary *Farmer,* of course — it became clear that his words was directed at me.

Well, I was rightly worked up, but you can't go hitting a preacher, leastways not in a church.

From where we was seated, we could not have easily got to our feet and walked out without causing disturbance.

Even when the service was over, we had to wait our turn to leave, as others nearer the aisle filed out slowly, while whispering to each other about what a fine sermon it was.

I held Mary's hand, the poor child clearly sad and embarrassed.

"It's alright, girl," I said quietly. "I reckon your friends went home early because they knew all that fool talk was coming."

"I hope so," she said, squeezing my fingers and bravely trying to smile.

But Georgina said nothing, spoke to no one, held her head high — indeed, my only indication she'd even heard the dang Preacher was the look of warning her eyes flashed at me once or twice.

At the edges of my hearing, I heard mutterings about us, from people not fit to wipe my wife's boots.

We were almost outside when the first insult caught my

ears proper. It was about me, so I didn't much care, having been called worse by better men.

That one began with a child asking innocent questions. "But why *do* people care, Father? You'd think they'd be happy. Isn't Lyle Frakes a famous lawman, and some sort of hero?"

"Perhaps he was when he was young," said the child's loudmouthed father, good and loud so we would all hear it. "Just a sniveling hiding-out coward now he's an old man though."

Georgina placed her hand on my arm, but she need not have done so. I only *smiled* at the fool man — and it was such a nice *friendly* smile, his eyes widened with fear and he scurried out of my sight.

Doesn't matter, there's always been fools, and there always will be.

But it was the next thing I heard that raised up my hackles.

As we stepped down into the street, not five yards to our left I heard the wife of the town butcher say, "Well, *I* heard he found his wife working a bordello in Deadwood, right before they came here a year ago. It's *said* she charged twenty dollars each time, and made an absolute fortune."

The woman and her friends laughed like simpletons, and her husband, Joe Simpson spoke up then, loud as he could, while looking right into my eyes. "Oh no, my dear," his voice boomed. "That's not how it was, not at all. The truth is, she loved cat work so much she charged the men only a dime! *Georgina the keener* they called her, she was quite famous for it!"

Well, insults is insults, and vermin is vermin — and when the first comes outta the mouth of the second, it's natural for fists to start flying, and that's what mine did.

The raucous laughter of the heavy-muscled butcher and his friends turned to shrieking and howling, as I bounded across and threw my first punch at his face.

He was lucky, for just as I threw it, one of his slack-jawed friends had doubled up forward with laughter at his unfunny joke — the man got in the way of my arm, misdirecting my punch enough so it went awry. This had the effect of me losing my footing a little — I stumbled sideways, tripped on someone's feet, almost fell.

Joe Simpson was perhaps only thirty, over-large, over-strong, over-stupid — way butchers so often are — and I reckon he fancied his chances. Most likely still thought of me as quiet old Kit Farmer — *but I ain't Farmer, not really, I'm Lyle dang Frakes.*

As his wife and her friends commenced shrieking, I stumbled into the midst of their group, and the butcher took advantage of me losing my balance, threw a wild right fist at my head.

My left ear sure rang from that punch. Not too bad at all — for a butcher — but fists ain't much use on a head like mine, it being just about solid bone. He'd be needing his butchering knives if he hoped to stop Lyle Frakes.

I squared myself up on my feet, nice and light and ready to dance[1]. Smashed a vicious right into his ribs, then a left to his solar plexus, which caused him to wheeze like a man who's been shot through a lung.

As the loudmouth doubled forward, all the breath

59

knocked out of him, I loaded my right fist with all of my weight; smashed it upways through the point of his chin; then watched him crash to the ground, out as cold as a new-buried corpse in a Montana boneyard.

---

1. DANCE: In the West, this often means a fight, using fists, elbows, chairs, or other fun things. Sometimes there's guns, which turns it into a dance of a more serious nature, and likely ends up being a whole lot less fun.

CHAPTER 11

"LOCK HIM UP...!"

"**A**rrest this man!"

"He's beaten poor Joe Simpson unconscious!"

"We don't want men like this in our town!"

"Lock him up, Marshal Rollins!"

Such cries went up all around me — but no further violence was forthcoming.

Truth is, I was more worried what Georgina would say, than anything Rollins might do. But right then I could not see my wife, for a crowd had gathered around to witness the fight.

"I do believe you are correct," Rollins called loudly, so everyone heard it. "This man *should* be locked up."

I turned toward him to complain as the townsfolk all nodded and shouted in agreement with Rollins.

He had to raise his hands in the air and shout, "*QUIET!*" to get them to stop.

"Marshal," I growled. "You heard what the man said 'bout my—"

"I said *quiet,*" Rollins yelled. "That means you too, Mister Frakes."

"Yes, *sir,*" I said. "You're the Law."

"Yes, I *am,*" he replied, then he looked all around him as he went on. "All you townsfolk hired *me* to do a job, which is to keep the peace around here. I'm hardly what you'd call experienced — I'd only ever worked in a hardware store, before I came here two years ago and was offered this job. Most of the time my job's easy. We have a lovely, quiet little town."

"Used to be," one of the butcher's friends said.

"Until *he* caused all this trouble," said another.

The butcher was awake now, I noticed, but Rollins ignored all a'that and went on with his speech.

"You townspeople want an arrest?" The Marshal's voice had a bite to it now, and I could not help admiring him just a little. "Because I have to tell you, I heard every word that was said, and I am *disgusted* with some of you people. Way I see it, Mister Frakes here showed restraint. If Joe Simpson — or anyone else — had ever said that about *my* dear departed wife, I honestly believe I would shoot them. So if you want someone arrested, just say so — I'll arrest Joe Simpson first, and anyone else who supports him." Rollins looked left and right, defying them all to speak up. "Well? Anyone?"

I nodded my thanks when his gaze fell on me, but I did not say anything.

"The job I get paid to do here is usually easy," he said. "I'm the first to admit that. But now it's time I earned my money. There are killers around, that's a fact we must deal with *together.*"

There was more mumbles, but still no one interrupted.

"Many of us have known the Farmers a year now — Kit Farmer; his wife Georgina; their daughter Mary. They're the same good people they were, before all of this happened. It's only their name that has changed. Lyle Frakes is a man who's done Law work most of his life — protected communities such as this one, before he retired — and having then married, he changed his name to protect his family. He had every right. Earned it."

"But those killers," someone from the back called.

"Lyle Frakes didn't *ask* those men to come here — by changing his name and keeping that a secret, he *avoided* that, don't you see?"

There was a few murmurs, but no one spoke up, so Rollins went on.

"I won't arrest Joe Simpson right now — but you're *all* on notice. If I hear of *anyone* spreading lies or falsehoods in this town, I'll lock them up for three nights — I mean it, man, woman or child, it's three nights in the jailhouse, and you won't like my cooking, I can guarantee that much."

Nice touch, that, I thought. *A Marshal's food would make me think twice, I've had such fare before, and ain't never enjoyed it.*

"People, please," he went on. "No one's asking you folks to help, but I won't have you making more problems. Mind your own business, people. And let the Frakes family mind theirs. They've done nothing wrong." Rollins looked around at the townsfolk while allowing his words to sink in,

then he fixed his gaze on the butcher. "And Joe Simpson —
you'd best apologize."

Simpson had been helped to his feet by now — he was
leaning against a pole for support, and gingerly touching his
jaw. Looked none too healthy. He stared back at the
Marshal while he thought some about it, and the silence
grew longer and longer. Then his gaze switched to me and
he grudgingly mumbled, "Guess I'm sorry. It was only a
joke."

"You *guess* it?" I said. "Real men don't *guess* when they
make an apology, Simpson. You stay outta my way."

I stared him down til his eyes dropped. Then I shook
my head in disgust, turned away from the big weak skunk,
started walking. The crowd parted before me, folks
seeming right anxious to get out my way, all tripping over
each other in their hurry to do so. Nobody spoke.

Georgina and Mary were waiting for me, both already
sitting up on the box seat of our wagon.

I winked at Horse, then climbed up beside them.
Georgina smiled at me with her eyes, continued to hold her
head high, placed her hand on my arm.

It was time to go home and prepare for the war that was
coming.

CHAPTER 12
CUT-THROATS

That night was quiet enough, mostly — all except for exactly at midnight, when three shots was fired from not far away.

Bang ... then a five second pause ... and *bang-bang*.

A younger man mighta gone outside, tried to chase down the fellers who'd fired them shots — but an older man has the sense to stay inside at such times, and wait for some daylight.

Having patience is partly how I got to be old in the first place.

And besides, I knew who it was, and that it was a game.

And it was a game I would play — but only on MY terms.

The next day was Monday, a school day. I wanted to keep Mary home, but she wanted to go to school, see her friends — their parents had dragged them away yesterday, but at school she hoped things would be different.

Georgina took Mary's side.

But instead of allowing Mary to ride alone to school on Dewdrop as usual, I insisted on all three of us going to town together — not in our heavy buckboard this time, but in our small buggy.

"I need to go in anyway, to speak to the Marshal," I said. "And the three of us should stick together til these Prewitts is dealt with."

It was a quiet trip to town, no sign of Prewitts. A little mist in the low parts like most every morning, and a real nice sea-breeze whistling through the trees. Perfect late-summer morning, aside from the possibility of skunks who wanted to kill me — but then, I spent most of my life with such threats around me, and I weren't dead yet.

I told Mary we'd be there to pick her up from school when it finished, and we watched her walk down the path to the schoolhouse, before driving the fifty yards down the street to see Rollins.

The Town Marshal's Office was small, just a small brick building with an office, a cell and a storeroom. Didn't need more than that, as the job came with a family-size house and stables, all situated next door.

I would have preferred for Georgina not to hear the things I had to say, but I also did not want to let her out of my sight.

Deputy Luke Golden's horse was tied to the rail out front of the Marshal's Office. We clomped up the steps and I opened the door, then followed Georgina inside and closed it behind me.

Golden jumped to his feet when he saw us come in, politely greeting Georgina and myself — with a nod and by saying, "Good morning" — but there sure weren't no kissing of hands.

His shiner had faded to a *light* purple now, his youthful good looks temporarily spoiled by that and a slightly fat lip. He was shaved clean, not a hair outta place, and even his clothing was neatly pressed.

Looks more like a big-city lawyer than a Federal Deputy, what's the world coming to?

Georgina smiled warmly at Golden, and just as warmly at Rollins. "Thank you," she said to Sam Rollins, "for what you said yesterday to the townsfolk. It could not have been easy."

"Only doing my job, Ma'am," he said.

And while Rollins was still not a man I'd want with me when things became dangerous, my opinion of him had risen this past day or so. He was doing his best.

I told the two men about the shots that were fired at midnight — and that I'd heard the same strange pattern of shots behind us on the way home from Los Angeles, not just once, but three times.

Georgina's eyes bored into me then, clearly unhappy I'd not shared my concerns about all that with her sooner. But she kept her mouth shut and listened — for now anyway.

"I know the Prewitts are camped in the hills somewhere not far away," Golden told us. "My main problem is that they're expert at hiding their tracks."

"Or maybe you ain't good at tracking," I said.

"Kit, behave," said Georgina quickly, tapping my sleeve.

But Deputy Luke Golden said, "No, Mrs Frakes, your husband makes a fair point. I do have *some* tracking skill, but a more experienced man may be able to find them. How about it, Mister Frakes? Will you ride along, help me to find them?"

They all watched me and waited for my answer. Years gone by, I'd have *already* been out there looking — and despite my personal dislike for Golden, I knew he was good at his job.

I have always said yes to such requests in the past. But I just can't anymore. No question about it. My life's not ONLY my own now. But it don't make the answering easy.

"No," I finally replied, and I heard my wife's sigh of relief. "Sorry, Deputy Golden, but I cannot leave my family unprotected."

"But Rollins can keep an eye on them while—"

"No, Golden, I'll watch them myself."

Sam Rollins spoke up — I knew what he'd say before it came out his mouth. "You don't trust me," he said, disappointed. "You believe me incapable, same as Sheriff Solomon Simms does."

"Did I *say* that, young Sam?" He shrugged his shoulders, and then I went on. "It ain't personal. I wouldn't trust any man alive to watch over them for me right now. Put yourself in my shoes a moment — you'd do exactly the same if it was *your* family in danger!"

The truth of that statement sunk into Sam Rollins, and he didn't sound disappointed no more when he said, "You're right, Mister Frakes. I apologize."

"And besides," I added, "if the Prewitts want to kill me,

they'll have to come try it on *my* terms. Not in their camp, where they've made preparations. No."

Luke Golden's lips curled a little, showing only a hint of his smugness. And his words only hinted at his meaning too. "You're not the same man you ... hmmm. It's alright, Mister Frakes, I should not have asked — you've been retired some time now, and to go after *tough* men, you'd need to be everything you were formerly *reputed* to be. I'll keep searching for the Prewitts by myself."

"I can help you," Rollins said. But Golden just shook his head, didn't even look at him.

"You shouldn't go alone either," I told Golden. "You seem like you got a good brain, you should maybe use it. Instead of chasin' them boys through the hills, you can wait where you know they'll be coming."

Golden scoffed at me. "Ha. You think they'll try to take Squirrel when he's being walked from the Los Angeles lockup to the courthouse up the street. No chance, he'll be too well guarded."

"Not then," I said. "Think, Deputy, think ahead some! Young Squirrel ain't killed anyone, the judge'll see that right off. So he won't be sentenced to hang."

"Your point, Frakes?"

"At the trial, I'll speak on behalf of the boy, ask the judge to go lenient on him. But when Squirrel refuses to speak, that judge won't be happy. He'll convict the kid of trying to kill me, and sentence him to a year. Maybe two if he's in a bad mood, but certainly not less than one. Now, anyone doing a year or more has to go to San Quentin, that's how this state works, no exceptions. So within a few days of the trial, Squirrel will be transported *there*."

Golden shook his head slowly, then spoke to me like I was a doddering simpleton. "And you *really* believe the Prewitt Gang will try to help him escape? They don't *care* about Squirrel — they're cut-throat killers, old man!"

Soon as he called me *old,* I felt Georgina's hand grip my arm.

"Deputy Marshal Lucas Golden," I said quietly. "I don't know what sorta family *you* come from…" I noticed he flinched when I said the word *family,* so I paused there a moment before going on. "…but I reckon you ain't got no brothers or sisters. If you did, you might understand *why* I believe they'll come for him."

He didn't flinch again, or react in any way strange. And his voice sounded calm when he said, "No, Frakes, you're wrong. The Prewitts are cut-throats!"

"The Prewitts are *people,*" I said. "Cut-throats, yes — but still *people.* When I was your age, Luke Golden, I made the same mistake you're making now. I figured all hard cases must be cold and uncaring. But wherever there's people, there's love — better hidden by some, but it's in there. Hell, they come all this way just to kill *me.*"

"You killed their family."

"I killed *one* of their no-good cousins. My three friends killed the others. And only to save our own lives when they came to kill *us.* Point being, these Prewitts know all that — but they had love for their cousins, and that's why they're here. They won't leave young Squirrel behind."

Georgina had been quietly listening, but now she spoke

up. "What if it's not love at all, Kit? What if it's pride? It's just something Mary was saying — something in a story she was reading, one of those long English novels. But perhaps it *is* true, perhaps revenge *isn't* always about love, but sometimes for family honor?"

Golden laughed loudly and clapped his hands together. And he looked right into my eyes when he said, "I believe your wife has you on that one, Frakes. Perhaps *you* aren't so clever as you thought?"

"Clever enough to listen to my wife and not argue," I answered, staring right back at Golden. "And yes, I reckon she's right, now I think some on it. But it doesn't change anything. Even if it's only for pride, the Prewitts *will* try to take back their own. Just as they done in Colorado Springs — their *pride* is what made them murder their own brother there. They'll come for young Squirrel, and you'd be a fool not to be waiting with a dozen good men, their guns loaded and ready."

CHAPTER 13

THE PERILS OF THE FAVORITE
MEAL

We spent the whole day in town, mostly making preparations. Got my horses shod and their feet trimmed by the good Spanish farrier, though they didn't really yet need it. I don't think he even speaks English, but he sure does know horses. I spent a good while in Rollins's barn, checked and greased everything on our small buggy, made sure it was in tip-top order.

No sense taking chances with killers about.

There would soon be a reckoning, and I would be ready.

We ate lunch at the restaurant, and while some of the townsfolk ignored us, a couple came and spoke to Georgina like things was all normal.

It would take time, but it was a start, and my good wife looked grateful.

We had never much known the Rollinses — I'd been careful to stay away from lawmen, as they are the people most likely to get suspicious of *who* a man really is — but that afternoon we got to know Sam and his mother much better.

To our surprise, Dot Rollins was a bright and lively companion. She was the type who always kept herself to herself, wore modest clothing, and in public, the woman never bothered using a word when a grunt would suffice. Yet in the comfort of her own home, she exuded great warmth combined with a razor-sharp wit — natural enough then, that she and Georgina got on like a pair of old friends.

And the meal she cooked us for lunch was as good as Georgina can make. I mean, *almost as good. Yes, that's what I meant.* And she was a wise one, I reckon. Told us not to worry, that the townsfolk would come around soon, see things how they really were.

I didn't much care what the townsfolk thought, that's the truth — but it *was* nice for Georgina to hear it from a woman she respected.

As for Horse, he had a fine time, just hanging about in the street, eating the flowers that grew near the schoolyard fence, and threatening to bite the young schoolteacher when he tried to chase Horse away.

"You should restrain this wild beast," called the teacher. "It's just not natural to let him run loose, he's an absolute menace."

Well, a'course I ignored him. I only tie Horse up when there's a good reason, and he never bites no one unless they deserve it. Wouldn't be fair to start tying him now anyway. Dang teacher was a fool.

Seemed like no time at all before we had to collect Mary from school.

From the hangdog look the child wore, she had not fared quite so well as we had.

"What's wrong, Mary?" said Georgina as the child climbed into her seat, holding back tears. "What is it?"

"Nothing," Mary answered. "Who needs friends anyway? I have horses and books, and two lovely parents, better than *anything* they have. And I have Princess Mayblossom too."

It had been awhile since I'd heard Princess Mayblossom mentioned — seemed like that rag doll had fallen somewhat from favor once Mary made real human friends, soon after we'd got here a year ago.

Anyway, for a first thing, Mary didn't wish to talk none about it — and for a second thing, she *certainly, absolutely, unequivocally, did NOT want me having a word with the other children's parents.*

Horse followed the buggy home, unrestrained just like usual, the clip clop of all my horses' feet pretty much the only sound. It *was* a little upsetting — we were used to Mary's chit-chat wherever we went, but today, she just weren't herself. But then, she has never been one to get locked in a bad mood too long — and by the time we came to our own place she was smiling again.

"I'm quite certain things will return to normal soon," she announced. "Once folks are used to our new name, and see we're still the same people we always were, everything will be perfect again, just wonderfully perfect, exactly as it was before. I'll just go on as normal, and make like nothing's changed, starting tomorrow."

"The day after tomorrow, you mean," I said. "Tomorrow's the court case in Los Angeles, remember?"

"But surely I don't need to be there," Mary said. "I simply *must* attend school tomorrow, it's—"

"Not safe with these Prewitts about, child. No, you can go back to school the next day, after the—"

"No!"

"Mary, don't speak that way to your father," said Georgina, and she placed one hand on my arm, and the other on Mary's. Then in a voice both quiet and wise she said, "We'll discuss all that over dinner."

Now, in my experience of marriage, when your wife takes that tone and puts off a discussion til dinner, it means *two* things — the first is, I'll be getting my favorite dinner, plus second helpings, *and* dessert. The second thing is, I won't be getting my way.

"Yes, mother," said Mary. "You know best."

I weren't gonna take it lying down, this being important for reasons of safety. I pulled my arm away from Georgina and said, "You was winking at Mary when you said all that, wasn't you?"

"Pardon? How dare you, Lyle Frakes. Stop this conveyance at once, I shall walk the rest of the way."

First thing is, my wife calls me Kit most the time, and she has ever since we was married. Only calls me Lyle Frakes when I'm in *real* trouble, and it's a sure measure of it. As for the second thing, threatening to *"walk the rest of the way"* ain't much threat when you're three-parts along your own driveway. Hundred yard walk ain't much likely to kill her.

I tugged on the reins and pulled on the brake.

So much for that fancy dinner, I thought. *I might shoulda waited til my belly was full 'fore I went up against my wife's wishes.*

Trouble with that, a full belly of his favorite things makes a man awful weak, and he always gives in.

Not this time.

I'll stick to my guns.

They *both* climbed down from the wagon without saying a word. *Both* held their heads high and haughty as they walked to the house.

Me, I just sat there and watched them.

Not Horse. Traitorous beast stuck his nose in the air same as they did, and walked right on by me, accompanied *them* to the house. I really should trade that dang double-crosser for a dog.

By the time I unhitched the horses, rubbed them down, put away all the tack and done all my feeding, it was just about dark. I'd spoke maybe two-hundred words at myself — not all of them cusswords, but most were — and I was in a ripe mood when I went for a wash before heading inside.

I expected to be roundly ignored, and to find myself eating cold beans from a can for my dinner — but to my great surprise, the smell of spicy roast beef assailed my senses as I strode through the door.

That's better, I thought. *Some respect. She's seen I was right all along, and is making up for it.*

As I sat at the head of the table, I breathed in the meal.

What a delight. Not just the roast beef, but Mary's fancy potatoes, all mashed up with butter-fried onions and cheese, then beans with cream sauce on a separate small plate, how I like it.

Only unusual thing, there was one extra chair at the table. It was piled with books, and on those sat Mary's dang doll, like as if she was planning to eat with us.

Even had her own plate, with small portions of food on it — exactly the same foods as we had.

"What's Princess Rustbuttons doing here?" I said.

"Princess *Mayblossom* told me she doesn't like eating alone, Father. But she's not really hungry, so perhaps *you* will have to eat her share."

"She should eat with us every night then," I replied, and we all tucked into our meals.

Smiles was worn wall to wall, and not a word was said of our previous argument. Indeed, the only sounds made were those of what Mary calls *gastronomic appreciation* — that is, right up until my mouth was filled with my second bite of that perfect dessert. Apple pie with sweet cream and cinnamon, if you must hear about it — your mouth's watering now, is it not?

Well, mine surely was — and a'course, my defenses was down — when Georgina said, "Now, husband, I have a suggestion. Unless you wish to feed yourself for a month, you'll listen to what I have to say while you eat your pie. After that, you may say what you like, but do *not* interrupt — unless your fondness for cold beans can stretch to a month. Maybe two."

I shrugged my shoulders, nodded and recommenced chewing.

"Kit, darling Kit. You're a wonderful man, and I *know* you only wish to protect us. But there are sound reasons why Mary will be safer at school tomorrow, instead of with us. And tomorrow is a *very* important day for Mary — she has a presentation, a project she's worked on for weeks."

I raised an eyebrow at the child and she said, "It's true, Father. It's all *anyone's* talked about at school these past weeks, and the whole day will be a special experience for *all* us children to share, I just *know* it will be! My own presentation is all about Australia. I told you about it, remember? You *must* remember? The maps, the kangaroos and koalas, and the platypus too, oh the platypus, such strangely wonderful animals! I've drawn *so* many pictures, remember?"

Thing was, I *didn't* remember — which just made me a low skunk for not paying attention when Mary prattled on. I mean, not *prattled,* but —hmm — when she *spoke enthusiastically to me.*

So I smiled at Mary and nodded my head. Looked back to Georgina, kept eating. Just like *any* father would do, if he had a lick of sense.

"I've thought deeply on this, Kit. About all the things *you* have told me. The Prewitts will know about the trial. And while they may not be such fools as to try anything, they'll be eager for news, and not too far away. You said it yourself, young Luke Golden should keep a sharp eye out, as they'll almost certainly send one of their number to town — though perhaps in some sort of disguise. *There* is where the danger will be — or on the trip home. And now that you know Sam Rollins can be trusted to watch over Mary, she's truly better off here."

I'd finished my apple pie — and I had to concede, she had made some good points.

"You shoulda let me teach the child to shoot," I said. "To protect herself, such situations, would be my main meaning. But you always said no to that. So, as things stand, I'm sorry, but I still have to say—"

"Beans," said Georgina sharply. And the smile she fixed to her face was so mean and tight, you coulda trapped animals in it.

"Please, Father," said Mary, grasping my arm and looking right into my eyes. "Australia! My presentation! I just know things will go back to normal once my friends see the wonderful pictures I've drawn. After all, who could *possibly* resist a koala? They look just like *you!*"

And right then, from somewhere, the sweet child whipped out a drawing she'd made of one a'them cute Antipodean bears — and she'd even drawn on a black hat same as mine, with a little blue band on it too.

What chance would any man have against two such women!

CHAPTER 14
AN ANGRY MOB

The air felt all wrong when I woke, day of Squirrel Prewitt's trial. But I couldn't work out why that was — I was missing something somehow, least that's how it felt.

I was up before daybreak making certain of everything I *can* control. That's all we can do, really, when it comes to it — be prepared for whatever might happen.

Guns oiled, good food in your belly, plenty of ammo at hand, spyglass in your pocket.

Georgina yawned when she came down for breakfast, told me I worry too much.

"Ain't worried," I said, handing her a plateful of bacon. "Only thoughtful. Someone has to be."

She had seen me this way, different times through the years, and knew enough not to interfere with the mood I'd put myself in. It's just part of how I get prepared, and she don't take it personal.

I still had no liking for letting Mary attend school today.

But Georgina was right — if there *was* to be trouble, it would most likely be in Los Angeles, or on our way back.

Most likely, probably, maybe.

Outlaw gangs are predictable, mostly. They just ain't clever enough to think through all the subtleties. Then again, one a'them Prewitts is a girl — and girls being cleverer by half, that one fact gives me pause.

Still, the decision had been made. We ate enough breakfast for an army to march on, climbed up on our buggy and headed into Santa Monica.

Town Marshal Sam Rollins met me halfway to town, and I gotta admit, he had a right serious face on. Still weren't who I'd *choose* to ride the river with, but his attitude was improving. Still a pear-shaped pen-pusher lacking experience, but his eyes seems more focused now. He might make a real lawman yet, if he lives long enough.

Anyway, he's all we got — no sign of that pretty-boy Golden. He'd be in Los Angeles already, helping the lawyer prepare the case against Squirrel.

A short while later we waved our goodbyes to Mary, and headed off to Los Angeles.

I had planned all along to drive in in the buggy — Prewitts would not expect that, most folks go on the train now. And if I need to get somewhere fast, I sure don't wish to be standing about, waiting for some train to get me there. You can trust horses much better'n train timetables, that's for dang sure.

But last minute, I did make one change. Decided to leave Horse behind. Normally I'd take him with me if there might be trouble — but some nagging doubt made me leave him behind just this once. He weren't happy about it at all — and what with him being the fence-jumping sort, I took precautions. Locked him up in Sam Rollins's barn, and promised I'd bring him a giant-sized carrot if he didn't kick down the door.

Disrespectful beast swore at me in horse language again — I was sure of it this time.

We had plenty of time, Squirrel's trial being scheduled for midday. So we clopped along nice and slow, saving the horses in case we had to get somewhere fast later.

Halfway into our trip, just after you pass by a copse of tall trees that look like they don't quite belong here, we stopped off at John Williamson's Livery. He's a short, lean, clean-shaved sorta feller, with a big ready smile, and missing both his front teeth. He's not only a good man with horses — he's a good man. Ain't a lotta folks round here I've warmed to, but Williamson's one.

And he never asks questions. At least, not ones he don't need to. I told him where we was going, and why, and rented two fresh horses from him. I had rented these two before — just to test them in case I might need them someday in a tight situation.

Perhaps on a day just like this one.

They were good horses too, a matched pair of strawberry roan geldings, so alike they just had to be brothers. Point being, they could drag my lightweight buggy at high speed the entire eight miles if needed — indeed, for speed they were a match for my own pair, at least at that eight mile distance.

It's mostly downhill from Los Angeles to John

Williamson's place, and they done it in 32 minutes the first time I'd tried it. I didn't hardly know him back then, and he'd looked none too happy when I returned them after the workout. But when I paid ten times the usual fee for the rental — and explained I would pay that amount whenever I took 'em — he had suddenly liked the whole idea much better.

And he was no fool — he could see I'd only pushed them as hard as was fair on the horses.

"Well alright sir, a'course sir, come back anytime you like sir." That was his attitude since, always happy to see me. Though he never actually called anyone *sir,* let alone a rough feller like me. John's a man who looks folks in the eye, and uses their name when he speaks to 'em. The sorta man you can trust.

As for them two fine horses of his, well they liked running hard too, stretching themselves some. Horses ain't made for only slow work — not good horses anyway. And that pair was as good a pair as ever got rented.

So we swapped my horses for his, and went slow the rest of the way, saving their energy for the slightly downhill trip home. Truth was, I was growing uneasy, and the minute I'd given my evidence, I'd be heading back to Santa Monica quick as two pairs of horses could get me there.

Despite our slow pace, we made it to Los Angeles with a half-hour to spare. Our plan was to eat a light meal before the trial began, but we went to the jailhouse first. Sheriff Sullivan Simms would be there, but I'd just have to put up with that — thing was, I wished to speak to Squirrel before the trial, make sure he knew not to lash out at the Judge or anyone else. The Judge would double his sentence if he acted wrong-headed — and I wanted that uppermost in Squirrel's mind.

But as we turned into that street, we saw men everywhere — all armed and milling about out front of the jailhouse. Perhaps forty men, all angry as bees at a bear. No women, babies or oldsters — but they too were anxiously watching as they cowered in doorways, or watched through shop windows, the whole town awaiting the spark that would set things afire.

"Whatever could have happened?" said Georgina.

Like as if I could know, was my first thought.

But I do know, was my second thought, right on the heels of the first.

"They've busted Squirrel outta jail somehow," I told her. "Don't get down off this seat, Georgina, no matter what happens. That there looks like a mob. And drive yourself to safety right away if there's trouble." I pulled on the brake, parked right in the street where we were, forty yards from the jailhouse.

"Everyone stop your yelling," Luke Golden was shouting at the men below from up on the porch. He fired a shot into the air, and added, "That's better," as they shut the hell up.

Then he looked my direction, saw me walking toward them and said, "Make way for this man, let him through. We need a man like him to help lead the posse."

A path cleared before me as I strode to the bottom of the stairs. I looked up at Deputy Luke Golden, and that dang skunk Sheriff beside him.

Golden looked into my eyes. "They busted him out, about thirty minutes ago."

He shook his head, almost imperceptibly. I knew what it meant. Guard was dead.

I looked from Golden to the other man on that porch — the man who *should* have been guarding such an important prisoner, morning of his trial. I stared into the man's eyes and said, "Where were you when this happened, *Sheriff* Sullivan Simms? And how the hell did they get in there?"

"I don't answer to *you*, Lyle Frakes," he growled. Skunk talked tough alright, but he could not hold my gaze while he said it.

"Lyle Frakes?" said a feller who was already drunk, as a murmur went right through the crowd. "Cain't be him, I met the man who kilt him in a fair gunfight, down by the Mexican—"

"Oh, this is he alright, the famed Lyle Frakes," Golden said. "The best tracker in the entire West, and a dead shot besides. And if Mister Frakes will track for our posse, we will surely put a quick end to the Prewitt Gang. How about it, Frakes?"

It had been said almost like a challenge.

I looked up at Luke Golden, and while the set of his face was serious — just as it should be when a fellow lawman's just lost his life — there was something else too.

His eyes had a gleam to 'em — almost like they was smiling.

It threw me some, I'll tell you that, as I tried to read young Golden's strange look — and I musta stayed silent too long, for the crowd grew some restless with mutterings and such.

"Please, Mister Frakes, come on up," the smooth-talking U.S. Deputy Luke Golden said. And he took one step down toward me, extending a hand — like as if I was frail, and needed *his* help to walk up the stairs.

I had no desire to do as he'd said — planned to dig in my heels and stay where I was, my main meaning — but at the same moment some fellers pushed me from behind. I sorta flowed right up them stairs, same way I get pushed to the shore by the waves in the ocean — difference is, I do *that* for enjoyment, and by my own choice.

I turned at the top of the stairs, stood between Simms and Golden. I looked over the still-growing crowd to make sure Georgina was okay. She was watching from the buggy where I'd left her — she raised one hand a little to let me know she was fine.

"Please, Mister Frakes," Golden said. "Will you do your bit? Help us bring these Prewitts to justice?"

"Ain't my business," I growled at the pup, who just raised his eyebrows, sorta-like to mock me, I reckon. The eye I had blackened with my fists still looked yellow and jaundiced.

"Just like I told you, Deputy Golden," shouted Sheriff Simms from a short ways beside me, where he leaned against the porch rail. "Old man Frakes is afraid!"

I didn't hit him.

"He cares not a whit about others," he shouted even louder, taking his hands off the rail to wave 'em about like some slippery dang politician. "These Prewitts came here to kill *Frakes* — yet *he* leaves all the dangerous work to the rest of us, and keeps refusing to help."

I didn't hit him AGAIN.

"See what sorta low skunk he *really* is, all you good people," Simms yelled, so loud now his voice hurt my ears. "Lyle Frakes is *yellow!* He ain't nothin' more than a filthy stinkin' old *coward!*"

I hit his fool jaw so damn hard, he crashed backways through the porch rail and into the street.

CHAPTER 15

"I'LL KILL YOU, YOU DAMN STINKIN' SKUNK..."

I 'll say this for Sullivan Simms, he mighta made some sorta politician — not the good sort that gets something done, but the sort that's good at whippin' up a crowd to get himself voted in, even though he ain't deserving.

When my fist sent him crashing through the porch rail into the street, he landed right on a few fellers who done their best to catch him. But the men next to them ones — those right in front of the stairs — advanced on me like a wild bunch, fit to do damage.

I was in for a beating by the looks, maybe even a lynching if things escalated. Anyways, it didn't look good, what with me having left Gertrude back in the buggy, and her little friend Wilma too — Wilma's a five-shot Remington Rider, in case you forgot. Tiny but useful, she's a real good gun in a tight sorta scrape. Normally Wilma would be in my pocket, but I'd left her in the buggy for Georgina, just in case she might need her.

Foolish of me really, as Georgina don't know how to shoot — and now I found myself unarmed in a bad situation.

No sense giving in without a fight though — and it would be sinful to not use the fists the Lord gave me for such situations.

As the first man reached the top step I landed a glancing right hook to his jaw, then drove a hard straight left through him, just below his right eye. He tumbled mule over turkey, unbalancing the fellers behind him, giving me the advantage.

But as I unloaded a thunderous right at the next man, Deputy Luke Golden fired his pistol — once, twice, and again — and everyone froze.

That is, everyone except for that second feller I punched — *he* went backways and downways, unconscious, his feet on the top step and his head on the bottom one. Funny thing too, his eyes was stuck open and staring, like as if he had died. Still breathing though — he'd be fine.

"I'll kill the next man who moves," Luke Golden announced. "And as many other men as it takes. You can *all* die today, if you'd like." Then he looked down at the feller nearest to him and, colder'n'death, said, "How about *you*, sir? Would *you* like to go first? That's the thing about being a Federal Deputy, I can kill whoever I choose to, it's part of the job."

Well, as chilling as young Golden said it, I knew that weren't true — but that other feller sure didn't. He raised up his hands, peaceful-like, and leaned back away, saying nothing.

"Frakes, step back against the jailhouse wall please," said Golden. "All you others, back away down the stairs, make room for your Sheriff."

I took only *one* step back — I ain't fool enough to get up against a wall without no space to move freely — and there was some mutters and such, but the crowd done what Golden had told 'em.

Simms had been helped to his feet, and was gingerly working his jaw with his left hand. It didn't look busted, but I knew I'd landed a good one — he'd remember me each time he ate, for a few days or so.

He looked at me, bitter-like, his right hand hovering down by his holster, but it was only for show. There was witnesses everywhere, I was unarmed, and Luke Golden was the man in control.

"Get up here, Sheriff Simms, please," Golden said, and Simms walked up the stairs. "Other side of me, not near Frakes."

I wanted to get going, get back to Georgina, go home, pick up Mary from school.

That was when I had my first clear thought since I'd arrived.

"I gotta leave now," I told Golden, staring into his eyes. "Prewitts could be halfway there if it's been a half-hour. My child."

"Don't worry about Mary," said the Deputy, calm as you like. "The Prewitts headed east, riding hard. That's how we know when it was — they were seen by some of these men."

"I seen 'em alright," said one farmer-lookin' feller.

"Me too," said another. "Ugly cusses, to a man."

It was clear they was telling the truth. The Prewitts rode east. But something about what was said just ain't sitting right. Still, this ain't no time to think, it's time to DO.

"I still gotta go home," I told Golden. "They *could* double back, and you know it. You'll walk with me to my buggy, in case this mob starts up again." Then I smiled toward the crowd and added, "Just so I don't have to hurt 'em, would be my main meaning."

Luke Golden shook his head, slow and thoughtful-like before speaking. "It's not safe to travel on your own anyway, Mister Frakes. Please, help us. You can go ahead, start tracking the Prewitts while I organize the posse. Sheriff Simms, take the names, we need to hurry." Then he called, "It's a dollar a day, men. And the knowledge you did the right thing by your neighbors."

"Dollar a day to get killed by some murderous gang?" said one a'them farmers. "Best thing I can do for *my* neighbors is get home alive and grow food, so as they don't all starve."

There was some murmurs of agreement in the crowd, along with some solemn nodding of heads.

Then his friend said, "I got a family to look after. Them Prewitts are bad men alright — and there's a good man with his throat cut inside the jailhouse there." He frowned and shook his head gravely before adding, "But good luck to you fellers that join the posse — I'll come along to your burials, say some nice things about you. And maybe, week or two later, I'll check in on your wives some, make sure they ain't lonely."

Them two moseyed along then and never looked back, and they sure weren't the only ones. Ain't nothin' like hard cold truth to take all the bluster outta some fellers. A minute later, there was just four men left in the street, and us three on the porch.

A few bystanders too, a'course, hanging back near shop windows and such, while they watched to see what would happen. Always plenty of those.

For some reason, Golden still sounded hopeful when he said, "We *are* short on numbers. You'll help us, of course, Mister Frakes?"

"No, young Luke, I sure won't. And I don't know why you keep asking, when you know that I can't."

"Afraid," Simms said — this time not loud, but under his breath and a little uncertain.

"You want something else 'fore I go, Sheriff Sullivan Simms? One lesson not enough for you?"

"You watch yourself, Frakes," he growled, then he spoke the next bit very quietly. "Once we're rid of the Prewitts, Deputy Golden will leave, and you'll lose his protection. I'd hate to see anything happen to you — or your *family*."

"I'll kill you, you damn stinkin' skunk," I cried, and knocked young Golden outta my way to get to Simms, who managed to dodge my first punch, but not the next three.

But as I stood over him, ready to finish him good, that dang U.S. Deputy spoiled things once again.

The familiar click of his six-gun and that smooth voice of his — "Mister Frakes, please, that's enough" — both rang loud in my ears.

I took hold of Simms' collar, dragged his face close to mine, stared him down one last time. And I whispered, "I'll kill you, no hesitation, if you ever go near them."

And I let him fall back to the floor, turned and smiled a warning at Golden, who kept the gun on me.

Then I walked down the stairs, headed back to Georgina.

From the frying pan into the fire.

CHAPTER 16
HOW SCUTTLEBUTT SPREADS

"Good luck," I said to the four men who'd been brave enough to join the posse, as I clomped down the stairs. "You boys best listen to young Golden if you hope to stay alive. Unlike Simms, he ain't a damn fool."

I strode back to the buggy, ignoring the gawkers, and climbed up onto my seat.

"You should not have done that," said Georgina, as I released the brake and reined the rented horses forward.

"Simms only got what he earned."

"I thought you'd calmed down this past year, Kit, but you're worse than ever."

"Enough!"

"No," she replied sharply. "You not only attacked *another* lawman, this time you threatened to kill him! I heard you from here, Kit. Look around you, there must be fifty people who heard what you said."

As we drove along the street, I saw she was right — all

types spying and gawking, from shopkeepers hiding in doorways to old biddies congregating in small huddles every street corner.

My threats against Simms would be spoken of all through the city before the day finished — the news of an escape and a murdered guard would ensure the whole story would spread — and in the same breath, those same folks would be saying that Lyle Frakes is a coward, refusing to help good ol' Sheriff Simms hunt down the outlaws.

You just can't win some days.

As we drove past the jailhouse there was no sign of Sullivan Simms. I saluted young Golden, and nodded at the four men who'd joined the posse. One slowly nodded back, looking pleased with himself — hard man by the looks. Bearded, heavily armed, and wore his hat low. Times must be hard if such men are happy to risk death for a dollar a day — or perhaps they just like the idea of hunting other men, and killing them legal-like.

The war left too many of that type, but they won't last forever.

We took two left turns, and headed out of town toward home.

Los Angeles was a bustling small city — fools crossing the roads every which way, buckboards parked in the streets without care, and everywhere you looked was the general mayhem of a prosperous place. I had to go slow til we made the outskirts of town, so as not to run anyone down, or injure our horses. I would soon make up for that though, and once we got moving, the wind would be loud in our ears, preventing clear listening.

So, in sight of the edge of town, I said, "I'm sorry, Georgina, I'm trying to behave best I can — but that skunk Simms made threats against Mary and you."

"I didn't hear any."

"Spoke them words quieter — not like he'd announce such threats loudly."

"The way you did?"

"Point taken. But he *did* say the words."

"Both times you hit him?"

I shrugged as I admitted the truth. "Only the second time. The first time, he'd called me a coward. I couldn't just let that go, could I?"

"Alright, Kit, let's move on. I take it the prisoner killed the guard and escaped? I heard some, but not everything."

"Young Squirrel's no killer, Georgina," I said, as we came to the edge of the bustling town. "Some of his gang come and busted him out. Simms shoulda been there himself, and..."

She grasped my arm tight then, looked up at me, sounded fearful. "What is it, Kit? You just stopped mid-sentence, why? You've realized *something*, what is it?"

"*Some* of the gang were seen riding east. Only *some* of 'em. '*Ugly cusses to a man,*' was how they was described by the witness. And no woman mentioned. Dammit, I *never* felt right about this. Hold onto your hat now, Princess, these here horses can fly!"

CHAPTER 17
GONE

Them horses sure burned the breeze.

I never bothered to look at my watch, when we skidded to a stop at John Williamson's place. But if that first eight miles took more'n thirty minutes, you can feed me horse dung for dessert, and I'll chew every bite.

Twenty-eight minutes, more like. Good horses, but they'll need a few days to get over the trip.

I leaped from the buggy, pushed fifty dollars into the wide-eyed hostler's hands, and cried out, "Help me, John, quick!"

"What have you done, robbed a bank?" shouted Williamson. "These horses are—"

"My daughter's in danger, John!" was all of my answer. And good man he is, he didn't waste no more moments.

"You think some of the Prewitts have killed Mary," said Georgina, as I quickly unhitched John's horses, and he ran to fetch mine. "That's what you think, isn't it? Please, no, not that."

"Not killed," I shouted back. "They'll keep her alive, draw me out. It's me they've come to kill. But we do have to hurry."

"I'm not a fool, Kit," she called back. "It's just like what happened with me, when I was eighteen."

I glanced her way, saw her utter despair. For she knew — she knew how these things went. Forty-one years it had been, but she'd never forgotten a single detail of it. Her own father had been killed that day, and I had been shot, my first time. It changed the whole course of our lives — and not for the better.

"How can I help?" John Williamson asked as we hooked up my horses.

"You can help me by staying alive," I replied. "Trust no stranger today, unless it's a young Federal Deputy, name of Luke Golden."

In no time we'd hooked up my own horses, and they took off like cats that's been scalded.

Reckon I owe John fifty more, now I think further on it. Well, he'll just have to wait, I got big fish to fry. Six rotten damn outlaw fish — perhaps even seven.

Georgina was right to be afraid, and I knew it — we might not survive this. If they *had* taken Mary, and if even *one* of 'em was clever, the odds were stacked chest-high against us.

The woman, I thought. *One a' them damn Prewitts is a woman. I should have been more prepared. She's outsmarted me now.*

She's taken my little Mary.

I feel it in my dang bones.

When something big happens, there's different ways men react. Some fellers, they go all to pieces — while others stay cool and start planning. Me, I'm mostly the latter. But when it's a loved one in danger — and you ain't right *there* to *do* something — even the coolest of men goes to pieces a little.

Then there's demons to fight, the worst kind — not evil men, something worse — evil thoughts, the type where you doubt yourself.

Them sorta thoughts, they're hard to fight.

That first half of the trip — til we swapped out the horses — those was the thoughts I was having. The time went by like the scenery did, all a blur, and my thoughts was all useless.

But after we left John Williamson's place, my mind settled in to clear thinking.

This was just how things were.

I would do what I had to.

If Mary was indeed gone — and she would be — I would track down the Prewitts, and I'd get my little girl back, I'd bring her safe home.

The miles flew by, as my horses' thundering hooves brought us closer to home, their speed not diminished by hills or rough ground, these horses doing what they were trained for — just as *I* would do what *I* have trained for, in the difficult days that would come.

Would they have killed Rollins, who I'd left to guard Mary, then taken her somewhere away? Or would them skunk Prewitts be waiting for us on the trail?

If they were truly clever, they'd meet me out here, rely on my thinking being unclear, bait me into a trap.

No, Lyle, they'll want their whole gang there — and some of them rode east a ways to lead you astray, give them time to go somewhere else. Time to set something up. You'd have seen that right away, even a year ago, you old fool.

Dammit.

I'm outta practice, my instincts have rusted.

I wish I could truthfully say I'm possessed of a calmness, a duality of mind, that allowed me to drive my horses so skillful and fast, while weighing up possible plans at the very same time. But the truth is, these horses a'mine don't need any driving — they've been trained for this moment, and knew just what to do. Every stride, every turn, every branch and rock they avoided, was all their own doing.

Me, I just hung on, sat on my rump, set my mind to clear thinking.

First time I had to give the horses direction was when we came to our own little town, Santa Monica — and there, I took up the reins, steered them to the schoolhouse.

As my brave horses swung hell-for-leather around the last corner, a rider came just as fast from the other direction.

It was Town Marshal Samuel Rollins, his pear shape unmistakeable, his horse flecked with foam from hard riding.

Georgina cried out when she saw him, a great cry of anguish and pain — and I had to restrain her, for she tried in that moment, unthinking, to leap from the buggy.

Our child.
Our child was gone.

CHAPTER 18
MY FAULT ALONE

Rollins pulled his horse up outside the schoolhouse the same exact moment I pulled on the brakes. All our horses was blowing fit to bust.

Georgina jumped from the buggy, the schoolteacher came out the door, and Rollins dismounted.

"Where is she?" I yelled at Sam Rollins. "Why weren't you here guarding the child, you fool?"

"Tom Trapp heard shooting out at the Grenville place," said Sam Rollins. "He rode hard as he dared the three miles to tell me, said he valued his life too much to go near it himself. Said it sounded like a full-scale war. I *had* to go, Lyle, you know that."

"Dammit!"

"Language!" shouted that damn young schoolteacher Hutton.

"I'll give *you* language, Paul Hutton," Georgina cried. "Where the hell is my daughter?"

"How dare you speak—"

"Everyone, all shut your traps now," I cried. And with a quick glance at my wife I added, "Please. It'll go quickest if we all take turns. You first, Hutton. *NOW!*"

"Why, Mary went with the woman you sent to retrieve her, of course."

"Dammit."

"Please, Mister Frakes, the children will be listening to us."

"But why *would* Mary go with the woman?" said Georgina. "We've taught her *never* to—""

"The horse," I said. *I had thought this all through as I drove.* "The woman brought Mary's pony, is that correct, Hutton?"

"Why, yes. Just as you'd requested her to. She said you'd sent her to collect the pony and Mary. And that she was to take the child to Los Angeles, as the trial was delayed until tomorrow."

"Rough type, this woman?"

"No, Mister Frakes, not at all. The opposite, in fact, stylish and quite ... well, appealing. But then, surely you already knew...?" He looked flummoxed a moment, blinked hard, then went on. "The woman was perfectly *decent* — indeed, when Mary lamented that she hadn't yet made her presentation, the young lady asked if Mary might be allowed to take her turn right away. To which I agreed — although it is *highly* irregular. Still, the child's drawings were excellent, except for the koala, which she had drawn wearing a hat for some obscure reason, and not just a hat, but also—"

"Woman came here alone? What color horse?"

"Yes, quite alone, sir. The horse was brown, I believe, just as *most* horses are. Yes, it was brown, not gray, I'm quite certain of it."

Fool thinks horses are only two colors. "Which way did they go, Hutton, quick?"

"Why, east of course, in the direction of Los Angeles, exactly as you would expect, sir. Is there something wrong? Did the child not—?"

"You fool," cried Georgina, and I had to restrain her, for she lunged at the schoolteacher then with intent to do damage.

"Ain't his fault, Princess," I said, and she spun toward me, sobbing against my chest and gripping me tight. "Mister Hutton was tricked, just as we were. So was Rollins — no one there when you got to the Grenville place, Sam?"

He shook his head ruefully. "Old Man Grenville was tied and gagged in his barn. His wife had been taken. Just the one man. We kept hearing shots up ahead. Followed the tracks for five miles, found her tied to a tree but unharmed."

"She say anything useful?"

"She said the man never hurt her, and seemed to think it amusing. Shots started up again then, maybe half mile on — and I fancy I heard someone laughing. Remembered then about Mary, realized I'd been tricked, and cut dirt[1] getting back. I'm sorry, Lyle, I let you down."

That teacher, he always *had* thought he was clever. But as he put two and two together now, he looked worse than stricken. "Oh no," he said. "What have I done?"

"Not your fault," I told him. "This is my fault alone."

And I turned away from him, carried my sobbing wife back to the buggy. "Rollins," I said, lifting Georgina up onto the seat. "How much head start do they have?"

"Little over two hours."

"I'll go saddle Horse and get after 'em. I need to start tracking right away. I'm trusting you, Sam. No mistakes. You'll keep my wife at your place and protect her til I return."

"No," Georgina squealed. "I'm coming with—"

Right then, Paul Hutton called out to me. "I'm sorry, Mister Frakes, I very nearly forgot. The lady who took Mary — her name was Eliza — she told me she'd left a clear message for *you,* with old Mrs Rollins. *A clear message,* that's how she put it. I thought *that* was strange."

I turned to tell Rollins to hurry — but he was already running.

_____

1. CUT DIRT: To run or ride fast as you can

CHAPTER 19
MARY'S NEW FRIEND

Hello, I'm Mary Farmer — no, sorry, I'm now Mary Frakes, I almost forgot. Perhaps you'll remember I told a part of our first story? The one where Father saved me from all those bad people last year? (Well, he always says I saved him!) I was Mary Wilson back then, of course.

All three names are important to me, and always will be, whatever the future holds for my family.

But whichever name I use doesn't matter. What matters is what we *do* — not what we say, or what someone else calls us, that's what Father tells me, and he's right. And I'm *much* more grown up now, not the child I was a year ago when you first met me. I'm ten now, and *much* more mature.

When Miss Eliza came to the school, I was suspicious — as Father has trained me to be. But she was so pretty and nice, so polite and so lovely, I believed what she said, which was only that Father had sent her to fetch me.

Well, to be honest, I did not *completely* believe her until I saw my dear Dewdrop outside, all saddled and ready.

It's *just* what Father would do, if he sent someone for me. He knows I would always prefer to ride Dewdrop, than sit in some tiresome rickety wagon or a loud smoky train.

Also, Miss Eliza batted her eyelids at Mister Hutton, and his face went redder than beet juice, then he mumbled a sort of a, "Yes, miss, of course, miss," without even thinking it through! *And* I was allowed to do my presentation right away, so I wouldn't miss out! My friends all seemed to like it, that was the most important thing. And Mister Hutton said it was *excellent,* except that koalas don't wear hats *or* carry guns.

Well, of *course* I knew that already — perhaps there's a rule against teachers having fun imaginations. Mother certainly believes so, at least in Mister Hutton's case. *It's called whimsy, you silly man.* And besides, that koala really *did* look like Father, which was the point. The crocodile I drew looked just like Mister Hutton, but he failed to notice — not so very surprising though, is it? People only see what they *want* to see, most of the time.

But back to my lovely new friend, Miss Eliza.

We enjoyed the first part of our ride very much. It was quite a fast pace we went, cantering mostly, which was quite fun for Dewdrop and me, and only enhanced our good spirits. And whenever we slowed to a walk to give the horses a rest, why, we talked like we'd known each other the whole of our lives!

Indeed, Miss Eliza and I became fast friends in record

time. She told me she lived in Los Angeles, where she worked for Judge Adams. That explained why she was so nicely dressed, I supposed — a very important job must pay well, and she must meet such wonderful people, along with an occasional rogue of the very worst nature.

"Yes, I do meet some rough types," she told me with a laugh. "Some of the very worst rogues a girl ever saw."

I asked her, "Did you get to meet the outlaw Squirrel Prewitt? *I did!* And did you know Father shot him, but once they actually met he even quite liked him? I hope they don't lock Squirrel up in the jail too long, though I think they just might. What do *you* think, Miss Eliza?"

She laughed at that and said, "They may yet let him go free. Just something I heard."

"That's a relief, I suppose. If he's going to mind his manners in future, and not shoot at anyone else. My father says Squirrel might become a good man, if he gets away from his brothers. And he's actually *very* handsome!"

"Your father said Squirrel is *handsome?* Oh dear, Mary, how strange!"

"No, of course not, it's ... it's *me* who thinks Squirrel is handsome," I said. Then, realizing Eliza was joking, I added, "Not quite so handsome as Deputy Marshal Luke Golden. I think perhaps I'll marry dear Luke someday, he's *ever* so lovely."

Something about that surprised her, I think, for she raised her eyebrows a moment, then looked behind us. A bearded man was riding behind, catching up quickly, and he waved. Then Eliza turned to me, winked conspiratorially and said, "I agree with you, Mary. That is to say, I think Luke's handsome too. I might marry him first, then divorce him once you're of age, so we both get to marry him. Is that wicked of me?"

"A little, perhaps."

"Oh, Mary, don't be so serious, I was joshing you again. And if you want handsome Luke you can have him. Us modern women must stick together. Don't you agree?"

She smiled at me so happily then, it lifted my spirits quite wonderfully, and I guess I would have agreed to whatever she said — even if I disbelieved it. "Yes, Miss Eliza, I do believe that is true for *all* of us modern women." It felt nice to have such a clever, pretty new friend.

"Now, Mary," she said then, quite serious. "Whatever you do, don't mention Luke or Squirrel to my brother once he catches us up. That's him coming behind us — he's my half-brother really, and can be rather ill-tempered. He's the jealous type, you see, and I think he doesn't like Luke."

A half-minute later he caught us, and that's when things changed.

Men surely can put a dampener on friendships.

No sooner did Miss Eliza's brother catch up, than all our fun stopped completely. His name was Henry, and he was the serious type. He wore spurs on his boots, which Father says only poor horsemen use. It's hard to respect a poor horseman, and spurs seem so unnecessary and cruel.

I tried to be friendly anyway, him being Miss Eliza's own brother — but he only glared at me and grunted.

"Quiet now, Mary," said Miss Eliza, her voice short and gruff now. Then, seeing Henry wasn't watching, she winked at me and smiled.

Well, that was something at least.

I wanted to ask just *why* Henry was with us — and *why* he hadn't come to the schoolhouse with Miss Eliza. Indeed, I had several questions, but whenever I tried to speak, I felt *quite* trepidatious.

I disliked Henry, rather a lot. But what could I do?

Still, I would see Father and Mother soon, and Los Angeles is always such fun! I would ask if we might go shopping, and bring Miss Eliza along — but not her mean brother. Not *him*.

And then something strange happened.

We were almost halfway — we had gone past Half Way House, as it's called, but of course, that's not *really* halfway. Father says Mister Williamson's Livery is exactly halfway, so that's how I know. But we were halfway between Half Way House and halfway — that's too many halfways, don't you think? Anyway, instead of continuing along the main road, Miss Eliza turned off it onto a side trail.

"Oh no," I said, reining Dewdrop to a stop. "Miss Eliza, that's quite the wrong way."

"Move, little girl," said Henry from behind me. "It's a shortcut, we ain't got all day." And he slapped my dear Dewdrop on the rump, and made a loud noise to try to scare her.

Dewdrop didn't budge, which made Henry angry I think, for he growled his next words.

"Move the damn horse, little girl, or I'll shoot it from under you."

"Come, Mary," said Miss Eliza. "We're just going to

visit a friend on our way." Then in a harsh voice she added, "Henry, behave, or you know what will happen."

I turned to glare at that nasty Henry a moment — it seemed he'd been put in his place, and us women must stick together, after all. Then I signaled Dewdrop to move forward.

We followed Miss Eliza in silence, single file on a very narrow trail for perhaps a half- mile, before turning left onto a wider trail heading north. A half-hour later we came to a proper wagon road, and turned left again.

The signs indicated Los Angeles was five miles to the right, and Santa Maria two miles to the left — but if Santa Maria was a town once, it no longer existed. We passed houses and barns here and there, but all were abandoned. This area was orange groves mostly — though most of the orange trees were dead due to the drought that had recently ended — and I saw and heard no one at all.

Finally we entered a lovely and pretty little valley, with a creek just a yard or two wide running right through the middle. It could have been a thousand miles from nowhere, for the valley gave it complete privacy. And there on the side of the hill was a small clapboard farmhouse, pretty as a picture-book picture.

Three horses were tied to the rail out front, and as we came closer, three men came outside to greet us. One of the three was smaller, thin, clearly limping. And it seemed to me that he cowered away from the others.

And to my great surprise, the cowering fellow was someone I already knew — it was that handsome young outlaw, who went by the name Squirrel Prewitt.

CHAPTER 20
THE SICK SMELL OF ETHER

It coulda meant just about anything, that message them kidnappers left about Rollins's mother. But it sure didn't mean nothin' good.

I *can* tell you one thing for certain. When he figures his mother might well be in danger, even a pear-shaped pen-pusher can get his feet moving — and quicker'n you might believe.

Sam Rollins sure put in the licks[1]. Lucky for him his place was just fifty yards off. He might not have been in good enough shape to go further, the speed he took off at.

Straightened Georgina *right* out, when she heard what was said. Her wailing stopped, and clear-voiced, she told me, "I'll bring the buggy, you go.

Rollins's horse had already gone home to find water, and mine would be needing some too.

Within a minute all the horses were drinking, and all us people were in Rollins's house. I smelled ether, soon's I walked in. Sam had already taken the gag from his mother's mouth, and as he untied her she told us what happened.

"A nice-looking, very young woman knocked at the door," the old woman said. "Perhaps only twenty, extremely polite and well dressed. Riding clothes, not a dress — but stylish, a woman of quality, if you judged by her outfit. Why, I actually invited her in! She told me she had a letter for Lyle Frakes, and would I give it to him? *'You won't open it will you?'* she said to me, just like that. I assured her I wouldn't, and she said, *'No, Ma'am, I'm sure you won't.'* That's when someone else grabbed me from behind, put an evil-smelling cloth to my face, and that's all I remember. Oh no, Sam! The children! Are they—?"

"They're fine," said her son, his face a strange mix of relief and concern. "All at school, safe and sound. But … well, Mary's been taken. That woman took her from the school while I was investigating a shootout east of the town."

I picked up the letter, read it out loud so I wouldn't have to waste time with questions about it.

MISTER FRAKES.

WE DON'T HARM CHILDREN. SHE IS PERFECTLY SAFE. WE WILL LET HER GO HOME WHEN YOU SURRENDER TO US.

YOU MUST PAY FOR THE WRONGS YOU HAVE DONE.

COME ALONE. OR BRING ANYONE WHO WANTS TO DIE.

WE WILL LEAVE A CLEAR MESSAGE AT JOHN WILLIAMSON'S LIVERY.

PLEASE DON'T WORRY ABOUT MARY.

SIGNED

YOUR NEW FRIEND ELIZA.

Clear message, same wording again.

"Don't worry?" Rollins looked puzzled a half-moment. "Strange thing to say."

"I'll *worry* her," said Georgina.

"I'll need two days easy food for the trail," I said. "This could take time, and I can't risk making noise hunting. Mostly jerky will do."

As the women went to the kitchen for supplies for my saddlebags, I quickly filled Rollins in on what had happened in Los Angeles — just the bit about Squirrel and the guard, not the parts where I punched Sheriff Sullivan Simms. *Then again, he might have enjoyed them bits better, given how Simms had belittled him.*

The women came back, and I stood to leave then, but Georgina and Rollins both insisted I could not go alone.

Last thing I needed in my way was a woman who can't shoot — next to last was a pear-shaped pen-pusher who probably ain't much better. I said words to that effect, but I sugar-coated them some — didn't say the words pen-pusher *or* pear-shaped. And I added that *most* women can't shoot, so it weren't meant particular.

If women's eyes fired bullets, I'd have been shot to bits in a crossfire, right about then. Seemed like BOTH women took it personal. Feller just can't win some days.

"Frakes, I know how good you are," said Town Marshal Rollins, "and I know my own limitations."

"Talk quick if you must," I replied. "But I'm walking out that door in one minute to saddle my horse, and I'm going alone."

"All due respect," said Sam Rollins, "they outsmarted you, Lyle. Outsmarted us all, up to now. And there is my point, that woman is clever. This won't be all about shooting, it'll be *thinking* that decides the result."

"He's right, Kit," said Georgina. "Three brains are better than one. I won't be left behind."

"You will stay *here* where it's safe," I yelled at her, poking holes in the air with my finger. "And you'll keep watch over her, Rollins, I'm leavin' right now."

"Lyle Frakes," said Georgina, not just poking air, but poking my chest with her fingers — one poke for each word. Then she kept poking as she went on, once for every dang syllable. "You've never once raised your voice at me all these years, but you have done so ten times this past day or two!"

"But I—"

"Shut it! I know how you feel right now, and you *must* know I feel the same. But it's time to stop all of your growling and *listen* for once. You need our help!"

"If you'd only listened, Georgina, let me teach you and Mary to shoot when I wanted—"

"Kit, I know *now* you were right. But you being *right* doesn't change how things *are*. Let's go now, together, the three of us. We start from right here, where we are, that's all we can do. You can teach me to shoot on the way, I won't be—"

"Georgina, please."

"Kit. Oh, Kit, darling, remember — I've *been* where she is. I'm the only one of us three who's been where Mary is — who's been the one *kidnapped,* I mean."

"But it's different, you were almost eighteen. Mary's just ten years old, it ain't nohow the same!"

"Kit, you *must* listen," she said, her claws digging into my arms, her determined steely gaze boring into my eyes. "I *know* how Mary is thinking. She'll be planning to escape, watching for an opening, she's clever, never stops thinking."

"Clever enough to behave and wait to be rescued."

"No. That's not her way and you know it, she's wild like you. As clever as she is, Kit, she won't sit about on her thumbs. I need to be there, to make certain Mary doesn't get you *both* killed. So stop wasting time and let's move! Let's go save our daughter!"

———————————————

1. PUT IN THE LICKS: To hightail it, either riding or running as quick as you dare. Also called PUT THE LICKS IN

CHAPTER 21
HELLRAISER

Luck's a fickle mistress, and it ain't ever helpful to rely on it — but it averages out, more or less, and our turn had arrived. Sam Rollins had good spare horses, and his wife had also favored the same sorta small pancake saddle as Georgina did.

"I couldn't bear to sell the saddle," he said, "or her horse. She was already ill when we came — that's why we moved here, you see — but her riding had always meant so much to her. I'll be honored if you use her horse and saddle today, Mrs Frakes."

"Honored likewise," Georgina replied. "I only wish I could have met her."

I had all sorts of worries to worry on — but none was to do with the horses or riding. Georgina had been a hellraiser when she was young, but most especially in ways that related to horses. At seventeen she did tricks that'd curl the hair on a bald man — she'd canter a horse while standing on its bare back, or jump from one side of a galloping horse to the other, touching her feet to the ground again and again, all for nothin' but fun.

Her father — *bless ol' Murphy's soul* — not only allowed it, but actively encouraged all this derring-do.[1]

Wonder she never broke her neck, really.

Anyway, she had kept up an equine interest all through her life — less dangerous by comparison these days, but still — and Georgina loved few things better than the feel of wind in her hair and good horseflesh beneath her.

She had always out-rode me, that there's the truth of it — but recent years, I've had the best horse, which just about evened things up.

There weren't no sense riding hard, no sense wasting our horses from two hours behind. We might need to burn the breeze later, best keep plenty of horse in reserve.

I took a minute here and there to check the tracks. Those of Dewdrop were easy to follow, and I saw that Mary was accompanied by only two other riders — well, it had been just the girls to begin with. But it was clear where the third rider caught them up after four miles. I need not have checked the tracks, really — there was no reason to disbelieve the letter Eliza Prewitt had left. The Prewitts wanted to kill me — they would not send me the wrong way.

What they *would* do, is set up a trap. That trap could be anywhere between here and John Williamson's place, but more likely nearer the latter. They would want their whole gang there to see me suffer and die. But at least three — including Squirrel — had headed east from Los Angeles. One other had ridden east of Santa Monica — they would want to meet somewhere with plenty of time before we arrived, and freshen their horses up too, if they were clever.

And yes, they were hoping to all see me suffer, not only to die. This was about revenge, family pride, they'd all want to see it, all wish to take part. This gave me one advantage, I knew from experience — they would try to take me alive, not just shoot me off of my horse.

Suits me just fine. I do my best work still alive.

Not knowing where their trap would be, it weren't no use making plans. So instead, I spent the time educating my companions how important it was that they listen to *me,* and not their own thoughts, once the party got started. I taught 'em some signals — not only with words, but some whistles and hand signals too, for we might yet find the Prewitts before they found us.

Unlikely, but stranger things happen.

Rollins eagerly listened, but it seemed like my wife's mind was elsewhere. Could not blame her, a'course, but I hoped I'd not made a mistake by bringing her along.

We spent near ninety minutes riding to Williamson's place — ninety minutes on edge, ready each moment for the big wild dance to begin. Yet not a thing happened.

I feared for John Williamson's life, well a'course I did. But if he was dead it had already happened — and when we neared his place, I decided the Prewitts must surely be waiting, ready to attack.

"Wait here, you two," I said, halting just before the last bend. "You'll know what to do by my whistle."

Rollins didn't argue, just nodded and said, "Good luck, Lyle."

He might yet make a good lawman.

Georgina, of course, could not help herself — but she shut herself down as quick. "But you can't just ... alright, Kit, of course, you know best."

Guess she'd been listening after all.

I touched Georgina's cheek. With my eyes I told her what mattered, then turned away from her. Taking Gertrude out of the scabbard I said, "Horse, there might be a frolic — you know what to do."

---

1. DERRING-DO: Daring or heroic action. Brave action taken with no consideration for the danger involved.

CHAPTER 22

MARY MAKES A DECISION

I may only be ten years old, but I'm not a fool.

When I saw Squirrel I knew right away what had happened. Father was right. I should have gone along to Los Angeles.

So much for us modern women sticking together!

I tried to escape right away, well of course I did — wouldn't *you*?

"Go, Dewdrop," I cried, and she took off at a gallop — but we didn't get far. She's an excellent mover, and has a big heart, but her little legs aren't long enough to outrun a *huge* horse.

We tried, oh we tried, but that horrible Henry put his spurs to the flanks of his horse, and they caught us up in a few moments. As we galloped along, he reached for Dewdrop's reins and reefed them toward him. Dear Dewdrop isn't used to such awful mistreatment, but she did as he wanted, and we stopped almost right away.

Horrid Henry said some terrible words then — more

spat those words than said them — but I ignored all his cussing and said, "Let my horse be, you horrible man, and we'll come along quietly."

But he just swore again and led us to the cabin where the others were now all waiting.

"Mary, please," said Miss Eliza as we approached. She was tying her horse to the rail. "I promise, no one will hurt you. But you *must* behave. Can you do that for me, Mary, so we don't have to tie you up til your father comes for you?"

"I *don't* believe you," I shouted. "You lied to me, and to silly Mister Hutton, and you're all really Prewitts, aren't you? Hmmph."

"Damn child needs a good whipping," growled Henry, still not letting go of Dewdrop's reins. "And it'll be my great pleasure to—"

"Henry!" Eliza exclaimed. "You will do *no* such thing. Water the horses and tether them to graze out of sight. And don't speak to the child again, you're scaring her needlessly. We shall treat her with kindness, and I'm certain she will behave."

She hadn't denied that she was a Prewitt, but still, she didn't seem mean. Not mean to *me* anyway. So when she smiled and helped me climb down, I went along peacefully with her.

We walked up the stairs together, holding hands. The men sneered as they watched, but didn't speak — all except Squirrel, who said, "Hello, Miss Mary. I'm sorry you're mixed up in this."

The others all looked *just* like Henry, bearded and ugly

and mean — and one of them growled, "Shut your mouth, Squirrel, you useless damn piece of—"

"Joe," cried Eliza. "Language. She's only a child." Then she said, "Everyone else, inside now!"

There were grumbles, but no actual words, and we all went inside. Eliza and I sat down at the table, while the men all stood, leaning against the far walls, waiting for her to speak.

She looked into each face, one by one, then finally turned to Squirrel and said, "What happened, you're all beaten up? Tell me the truth."

Squirrel's gaze darted to Joe, who was standing close by on his left — Squirrel was half his brother's size, and he cowered away from him now as he struggled to speak. "It's from falling off the horse is all, Sis. When I got shot in the arm by Mister Frakes."

"*Mister* Frakes! You hear that?" growled Joe. "*Mister!* Damn fool kid seems to think Frakes is his friend."

Eliza warned Joe with her eyes, then went back to questioning Squirrel. "No, little brother, what you told me wasn't the truth. I was told you were fine, aside from a slight flesh wound to your arm. So why are you limping now?"

"I fell again, Sis, is all. While we was ... I mean, after the..."

He looked like he might cry, poor Squirrel. And Eliza didn't believe him, not for a moment.

She spun to face ugly Joe, and said, "What did you do to him this time? *And why?* I bet it's *your* fault he got shot, *your* fault he got jailed, and now you've beaten him too."

"He charged at Frakes's house on his own, the damn little fool!"

"Oh, Joe, you're a *terrible* liar! We all know Squirrel only *ever* does as he's told, he'd never have thought to do that by himself. You *told* him to do it alright, and just about ruined the whole plan! I've had quite enough of you, Joe, you just wait til—"

"Weren't my damn fault what happened at the jailhouse," Joe snarled. "Useless kid didn't want to come with us. Wanted to stay in the cells, if you can believe it! Lucky he didn't — way things turned out, he woulda swung for it."

Eliza sounded genuinely shocked. "Swung for *what?* What are you talking about? What did you do, Joe, you fool?"

"Weren't me! I ain't the one likes to use a damn knife. Rifle man, me, and you know it. You *know* who—"

"Alright, but *who?* Who was killed?"

"We got Squirrel out before daylight as planned. But the boss went back, killed the guard — reckoned the feller weren't to be trusted."

"Oh, no."

"No," said Squirrel, and his face fell. "That guard was a real nice—"

"Shut your mouth, Squirrel, this ain't—"

"Alright, stop it, all of you!" Eliza sounded hysterical now, and I must say, I felt that way too, all this talk of knives, as Eliza went on. "No more about that, Joe, I mean it. You're scaring poor Mary with your foolish talk. The truth now! Why *did* you beat Squirrel?"

"Had to make him come along somehow."

"But he was already out of jail. Surely you could have—"

"There was no other choice, he was starting to yell the hotel down. And don't threaten me with what the damn boss'll do when he finds out — he knows already. It was *him* who gave me the order to beat the damn kid when he wouldn't leave. I weren't about to go against a crazyman's orders, he'd likely have cut my throat too."

"Is all that true, Squirrel?" she said, clearly hoping at least *some* of it wasn't.

It's strange how a shrug of the shoulders can mean different things — it was Father who taught me that, and I've made a study of it since then. In this case, Squirrel's shrug meant that it was all true, but not *only* that.

It also meant he felt defeated.

Squirrel was still young, and had a good heart, unlike all of his brothers. He didn't *belong* in a mean outlaw gang, he just didn't. But as I found out when I was orphaned — back before Father saved me, I mean — there are circumstances in life we cannot gain control of. No matter how we try, or what our own beliefs are, some things are beyond our control.

And Squirrel, he was a Prewitt, like it or not.

It must have been AWFUL for him, to grow up in that family, every day of his life.

Father was quite right to *like* him, of course — and I hoped that he wouldn't kill Squirrel when he came to rescue me from the Prewitts.

Eliza, I wasn't so sure of, now I thought about it. She

seemed so very nice, but on the other hand, I had one nagging doubt — she *seemed* to be boss of the men who were here. I supposed that the *real* boss must be their eldest brother, and *he* was clearly not here — but why would Eliza be second in charge? Clearly, she was younger than *any* of them, except Squirrel, who was really, almost, still a child. '*Between hay and grass,*' was how Father described him.

He really DOES speak quite strangely — but I like it a lot.

And quite obviously, Eliza cared *very* much for Squirrel. And too, she was right after all — us modern girls *must* stick together. So I decided Eliza probably was just as nice as she seemed.

At least, I would trust her for now — 'more-or-less kinda,' as Father would put it.

It was an odd situation, but I wasn't too worried for myself — I knew Father would save me, he's done so before, several times. But I realized now, if he came here, he just might be forced to kill them *all* — not only the ugly brothers, but Squirrel and Eliza might get killed too. They were *both* too young to die, and also too nice!

There was only one way to avoid it — I would have to escape!

CHAPTER 23
THE VALUE OF SOMEPLACE
TO HIDE

Problem with Williamson's place, it had forest too close on one side. He shoulda built further from it, or cleared extra land. I must ask him sometime if he knows what them tall trees are called — I never seen such before, in all a'my travels. Might be they was brought across oceans from some far-off place. Strange, what humans do.

Anyways, them trees was within shooting range of his house and his barn, and that didn't sit well with me.

But then, I guess this part a'the world is these days less violent than the parts I been used to. Guess he felt safe enough, how it was. But maybe now, them days is over.

The air too, is different to my place. Thicker somehow. The heat crowds in on a man, and briefly, I shook in my boots. Fear? Just a healthy amount. Perhaps it was mostly the heat, made me feel so stifled.

Me and Horse entered Williamson's yard at a walk,

nice and quiet, all our senses stretched to their limits. But the place sounded dead.

Bad choice of words, I know, but that's just how it was. Even the insects was too scared to move. Not so much as the swish of a horse's tail, inside that still moment.

Anyway, like I said, it was quiet — too quiet in fact, and that's trouble.

Normal day, you'd hear Williamson himself, for he was a whistling sort. Always a tune as he worked, when things was all good.

Horse felt the wrongness of it too, well as I did or better. He moved slow and deliberate, ready to leap in any direction at the sound of a rifle being cocked, a branch being stood on, or a bird taking flight where it shouldn't.

Nothing.

And more of the same.

If we could make it to the barn without being shot at, we would have complete cover.

We went that way, slow, not quite straight, keeping the house between us and the trees where we could.

Hard to make your voice do your bidding, when it might spark something big. But it had to be done, and besides, I could not stand the quiet any longer.

"John? Are you here, John? It's only me, Lyle Frakes, on my lonesome."

The answer I got was no answer at all. Not a sound, not a puff of air moved in the still of the day.

We made it to the barn without being disturbed, but Horse, he was mighty uneasy. Ready, but he weren't sure what for.

We rode straight in through the open barn doors. There weren't no intruders in there, or Horse would not have gone in — I could trust him on that. The coolness washed over us like a great ocean wave. Or perhaps it was only relief.

Well, a'course it was both.

Like many buildings in this area, John Williamson's barn was old, with thick walls of adobe. I stepped down to the dirt and straw floor, let Horse walk ahead to drink from a trough of cool water.

"Well, there's something ain't right, Horse. If John was inside the house, he'd have come when I called him. I just hope he ain't—"

"I'm down here, Lyle," came a voice, muffled but definitely John's. "You'll have to take a step back, you're on top of the hatch."

Ten seconds later, John was standing beside me.

"Well if that ain't the best hidden hatch I never saw," I said to him. "Never took you for such a careful type, John."

"You might be less surprised if you knew what my real name was. Might tell you some other time — or perhaps best I don't. Some things are best kept in the past, as you yourself know."

"I'll drink to that," said I, as he poured us a small brandy each from a bottle on his workbench, and we both took a small sip of that fragrant thick liquid gold.

Oh yes, it was the good stuff.

"The Prewitts were here, Lyle. Announced themselves as such when they rode in. I'd seen 'em coming down the road, and thought of your words about not trusting strangers today. Took to my hole before they got to my gate."

"I'd best let Georgina and Rollins know it's safe to ride in, they'll be worrying their fingernails off. Won't take but a moment, might best close your ears from the shrillness." I stepped outside the barn, whistled a short one followed by a long one, then came back inside. "Them Prewitts search for you, John?"

"They did. Not for long. Called out that they'd seen me from a distance. Knew I was still here, and knew I was hiding. Said they was the Prewitts, with a message for Lyle Frakes. Said to make for the Monte Vista Road. Said they'd leave you a clear message between here and there."

I took off my hat, scratched my head some while I tried to think. "That the road leads from Los Angeles out to that failed township that sits below the mountain? Place with all them dead orange groves?"

"That's the place," he said, pouring us another. "Santa Maria, the town woulda been called, but the drought dried up all the water. Real quiet, no one living out there now. Folks say the place is unlucky, got an Indian curse on it maybe. It was about fifty blocks, each one-sixty acres, maybe ten of those with old houses — lotta choices for outlaws to hide, is my point, Lyle."

"If I'd been thinking clear, I shoulda guessed that's where they'd be."

"Anyway," Williamson went on, "that was forty minutes ago when they left. Stayed in my hole to be certain. They have Mary, don't they? I'll come with you, Lyle."

130

"No, John. But thanks for the offer. I had planned to take you along, if I'd come here alone. But to tell you the truth, I got too much help already, if you know what I mean."

"You could slip away, leave them two here," he said with a glint in his eye. "I could help you with that, then meet you uptrail a ways."

"They'd only blunder in later. No, I'll keep 'em close by me where I can limit the damage they do. John, listen. Do you trust the County Sheriff?"

We both looked out of the barn then, as we heard Georgina and Rollins ride in, and I beckoned them over toward us.

John Williamson rubbed at his chin, thoughtful-like. "Good ol' Sheriff Sullivan Simms? Hmmm. Popular, and a tough reputation."

"Not what I asked."

He shrugged. "Alright, it's a no. But it's a no you best keep to yourself. Thing is, Simms has a strong reputation for being incorruptible — but lately, strange happenings, way I see things. This place is no San Francisco, but there's plenty of money about. Big business, getting bigger too. Wherever there's money there's greed, and it spreads out to every dark corner, scoops up every dark heart in the end. Guess you got a reason for asking?"

"Ain't normal, a Deputy getting his throat cut, broad daylight, inside of a jailhouse. Night-time's one thing, but middle of the morning?"

"Witnesses?"

"Prewitts was seen riding west a few minutes after, but

not a soul seen 'em in town. And it seems to me like that Deputy would not have let a stranger inside the building. Solid adobe, that building, and only that one heavy door — still solid on its hinges, I checked."

"They built that door several years back, when they finally put a stop to the lynchings round here. After the Chinese massacre, if you heard of it."

"Damn disgrace."

"Lynchings all stopped once that door got built. That jailhouse might as well be a fortress. You're right, it doesn't add up, Lyle."

"Anyway, just some thoughts I was having. It mighta been the guard let 'em in, but my logic tells me it's Sheriff dang Simms. Don't trust him, John, if he comes here. Something ain't right."

It was time to ride north.

CHAPTER 24
MARY HIGHTAILS IT

"Get that damn little girl outta here," said Henry Prewitt when he came in from watering their horses. "We need to go over the plan again."

"What's *she* gonna do?" Joe growled back at him. "Run tell her daddy?"

The *ugly* Prewitts all laughed when Joe said it — not Eliza or Squirrel, they're not ugly at all. Then a different ugly one said, "Don't make no difference what she hears, she's seen all our faces."

Well, you would have thought Eliza was seven feet tall then, and had eyes that fired bullets. She leapt to her feet, ran at that big mean brother and slapped him a good one, right across his filthy bearded face.

As he grabbed her wrists she kicked at his shins and yelled, "Anyone harms this child won't live to see sunrise tomorrow! You all hear me, you rotten low skunks? It's not just *me* you have to worry about now! I've got *help*, if you fools have forgotten. And he *will not* put up with your—"

"Leave her be, Bill," said Joe. "We all got beards and hair enough to disguise us, and none of us got scars to speak of. It's only *her* face and Squirrel's the girl can describe if she lives. And they both been showin' their faces all about town already."

"That won't matter," cried the struggling Eliza.

"Take the damn child outta here anyway," said Henry. "That smile a'hers makes me uneasy. What's she got to smile about anyway? Maybe she's simple."

"I am *not!* Am I smiling *now?* And let Miss Eliza go, you horrible brute!"

"Shut up, you," he growled. "We're gonna tie you up on the porch."

Eliza broke away from the grip of that ugly brother, hurried to my side and said, "No one's tying you up, Mary. You may *sit* on the porch if you like."

There was uproar and argument about *that,* but it all stopped when I put on a *very* shrill voice and hurriedly said, "I'm sorry, Miss Eliza, but I really *must* use the outhouse. I mean, right away!"

"I'll come with you, Mary," she said. Then to her brothers, "We won't be a minute."

"It's not ... that is to say, it may take a *few* minutes or longer. What I mean is, I have to..."

I left the words hanging between us, and as I expected, the men all looked away. Seems even the meanest of men, those capable of killing without a second thought, become squeamish when confronted with the fact that a young girl uses the outhouse for the same reason they do.

"Well, we gots to go over the plan now," one of them

mumbled. "You too, Eliza. Send Squirrel to watch her, he ain't got nothin' else to do anyway, besides lie around bein' useless."

I tried to look completely offended. "I will *not* be watched while I—"

"I'll stay right on the porch while you go," Squirrel said, "and look the other direction, a'course."

This was just what I'd hoped for. Acting as demure and embarrassed as I could manage, I walked out the door after Squirrel. The outhouse was about fifty feet away, and I scurried across in a hurry, before turning around and saying, "It may take awhile, Mister Squirrel. It does sometimes when I'm scared."

He nodded, I went inside, and he turned away.

I didn't need to use the outhouse at all — *how could anyone, in such a situation?*

The door squeaked when I closed it behind me — but I didn't quite close it completely. I waited a few seconds, peered out the crack. No one else had come out, and the house had no window this side. And true to his word, Squirrel was facing the opposite direction, leaning against the house, rubbing at his sore leg.

Slowly, carefully, I opened the door — I felt the resistance, the heaviness of it on its hinges, and thought it might give me away any moment — but it didn't. I opened it up, not too far, as I'm thin, and can fit through a *very* small opening.

I slipped through the doorway, then pulled it shut with the same care. Taking the quietest of steps, I placed each foot deliberately down on the dirt, avoiding the sticks that seemed to be almost everywhere. In this manner, I sneaked around to the back of the outhouse, where I finally took a deep breath.

I was free!

Of course, I quickly worked out that there are several different degrees and definitions of free — and the extent of my freedom wasn't much. At least not yet.

What I *wanted* was Dewdrop.

But if I went near the horses I'd be caught for sure. I'd come back for her later, with Father and Mother, and the brave, handsome Deputy Golden, and that nice Town Marshal Rollins perhaps. It would be a wonderful adventure, just like those in the silly dime novels Father enjoys.

I still had to be quiet to begin with. But I thought that by keeping in a straight line, I could stay out of Squirrel's view until I got to the trees. Then I would find my way home, I was certain, by using the position of the sun as a guide, just the way Father taught me.

I had gone perhaps one-hundred yards when I realized, the smallness of the outhouse could no longer keep me hidden from Squirrel's view. He was *still* looking in the other direction, but I knew I could not have much time left.

I started to run!

I have always been a good runner, but the distance seemed terribly far and my legs seemed so short now — *this is how dear Dewdrop must have felt, being chased by that ugly mean Henry Prewitt!*

I ran and I ran, and it seemed almost like I went up and down on that one spot. But no, I *was* making progress! I was just fifty yards from the trees up ahead when I heard angry voices back at the house. "Damn you, Squirrel, she's gettin' away!"

I kept running on my little legs, my breath short and ragged, and I didn't waste any time by looking behind me.

"Stop, little girl, or I'll shoot," was the next voice I heard, and that voice was a mean one.

"No!" "No, no no!" That was Squirrel and Eliza.

"Give me that rifle!"

"Get her!"

"No!"

"Owww!"

Just fifteen yards to go!

Then a piece of the ground, in front and to my right, just exploded up out of itself — and then I heard the shot, and another, and another, as more ground exploded around me, and I started to cry.

"Father," I cried as I fell. *"Oh, Father, avenge me."*

CHAPTER 25

"MORE CLEVER'N YOU LOOK..."

We rode the trail north in silence at first. We was worried for Mary, a'course, but done our worryin' quietly.

But a short ways in, Georgina asked me about the things I'd said to John Williamson. In particular, my concerns about Sheriff Simms.

I told them everything, then Rollins said — off the record — that he didn't like it none neither. "Can't be certain, but I *believe* Sheriff Simms took a bribe from the Prewitts to help young Squirrel escape."

"But why would he?" Georgina argued, riding between us. "A respected County Sheriff like him, just a month before an election. His reputation is solid. I know you both have good reason to dislike the man — but it doesn't make sense to suspect him."

"Tell that to the feller with his throat cut," I said. "Anyhow, way things stand, we don't trust Simms if we come across him. Trust only Luke Golden until I say different."

"Sure changed your tune about *him*," said Georgina, with one a'them *knowing* sorta looks she's so good at. *"Haven't you,* husband?"

"I admit I made some mistakes in all this," I replied. "Too long away from the action has frazzled my instincts. But it's all comin' back to me now. Least I hope it's all back. Hard to tell, so much happening at once. But I'm *certain* Sullivan Simms ain't playing things straight now — I *feel* it, all through my bones."

Georgina proceeded to tell Rollins about my fistfights with Simms in Los Angeles. And how me and that skunk of a Sheriff had made threats against each other too.

"If Simms *is* in cahoots with the Prewitts," I warned them, "he might just meet up with us somewhere along this here trail. Him knowing their whereabouts, he won't have no trouble tracking them, would be my main meaning."

"Now *that* could be something of a reason," Georgina said, as some birds took to flight from a bush right beside us. "A reason for Sheriff Simms to do a deal with the Prewitts, I mean. He *may* plan to double-cross them, don't you think? He'll look *quite* the hero if he plays a major part in their arrest."

"I don't know," said Rollins, slowly shaking his head as he whistled through his teeth. "Is that enough reason for Simms to kill his own Deputy?"

"Maybe, maybe not," I said. My mind was already up ahead. "Thing is, I don't want no lawmen around when we get to Mary. Not even honest ones. He's good, Luke

Golden, but he's young yet. He'll want to shoot first, get Mary out later, and that could lead to her getting..."

I left it unsaid, but we all heard it, much too loud and too clear. We rode on in silence a ways, least a minute or more, til Rollins broke the silence.

"You'd best tell your wife the truth now," he suddenly said.

Might make a good lawman yet, I thought grimly.

"What truth? *Kit?*" Georgina grabbed my arm, and we all three pulled up our horses as she tried to read my face for an answer.

"Alright," I said. "Better now anyway, maybe, so you don't cause a problem when it's time. I'll be giving the Prewitts what they want, in exchange for Mary's safety."

Her claws sure dug into me then, and she spat the word. *"You!"*

"It's the only way," I admitted. "Once she's clear, I'll do what I can. There ain't no other way, Princess."

"But surely—"

"No. They'll shoot her for spite if I don't go in quietly. A hand or an arm — maybe a foot — but if I don't go right in, they'd surely do it. So this is the plan. Rollins will—"

"I *won't* be left behind, she's my child!"

"I know it," I said. "So as I was saying, if we make it to their hideout without any escort, you'll ride in with me to the meeting. We'll meet in the open, exchange me for Mary, then you and her ride away."

"Will they allow it?"

"Most likely. It'll be somewhere near an abandoned building, but the exchange will be out in the open. I won't be made to give up my gun til you're clear. That's a normal condition, such times."

"Alright," she said, with a nod of resignation. "And what about Town Marshal Rollins?"

I turned to Rollins, questioned him by raising my eyebrows, just to see if he knew.

"I'll be hidden nearby with my rifle — which I'll only fire *then* if there's trouble."

"Right so far," I said. "And once my girls ride away, and I go inside?"

"I'm to protect Georgina and Mary, make certain they get to safety, before coming back to try to help you, of course, Lyle. But I must take my time, even then, and wait for an opening. They'll be in no hurry to kill you — and once the daylight's gone it'll even things up some."

"More clever'n you look, ain't you, Sam Rollins? Get that from your mother, I expect. If you survive this, you might just make a good lawman. Just make sure you don't shoot my horse — we might need his help later."

Georgina looked like her face might just fall apart, but she held herself together and nodded a grim one. "So Mary and I should try to find Luke Golden and bring him to you?"

"Yes," I said, raising a smile from somewhere. "It'll be fine, Princess, you just do *your* bit, and leave all my bits to me. Never let you down yet, did I? Well, not this forty years recent..."

"No, Kit my darling, you've done your best for me, always. And I'll do just what you told me. For Mary. For you."

CHAPTER 26
MARY'S RECOVERY & SQUIRREL'S KIND EYES

I woke lying on an old bed, with dear Miss Eliza holding onto my hand.

"There you are, Mary," she said softly, as she wiped my brow with a damp cloth. "About time you woke. We were worried about you."

"How many fingers?" said Squirrel, putting his hand so close to my face it was all just a blur.

I pushed his hand away. It was cold. "Am I not dead then, Mister Squirrel? How many bullets are left in me? Did *you* cut them out, Miss Eliza? Do you think I'll live? I want my mother and father to come now. Tell them not to bury Princess Mayblossom with me, she's terribly scared of the dark. Oh, everything is so dark, this must be the end."

"Oh, Mary," said Eliza with a funny little laugh. "You haven't been shot at all. Joe fired near you to scare you so you'd stop running. You got your legs tangled, and must have hit your head when you fell."

"So I have a terrible head injury then?"

"Do you have a headache, Miss Mary?" asked Squirrel.

"Well, no."

"How many fingers?"

This time they weren't quite so close.

"Why, three, I believe, Mister Squirrel. Do you think I might live?"

"Three's right," he replied. "I reckon you'll be just fine."

"We're hungry," came a gruff voice from another room, and I realized where I must be.

A different voice then: "Get out here and cook something right now, Eliza. We need to eat our fill afore this gets started. You fussed about with that damn strange kid long enough."

"Bet she wants a damn kid of her own," said another voice. "Be a worse mother'n ours was, I reckon." I think that was Henry who said it, but I couldn't be certain. Someone very *mean* anyway, whoever it was.

Eliza told me she would come back to check on me soon, then she went out. She smiled at me before closing the door, leaving just Squirrel and me in the room.

"Sorry, Miss Mary," he said quietly. "I ain't allowed to give you no privacy now, on account of you running away before. It was Bill who punished me this time. They take it in turns. Guess it split fair this time though — I shoulda known you'd try to escape. Well done too, by the way, you just about made the trees."

"Thank you!"

He handed me a tin cup, half filled with water, and I drank it as he went on. "I'm kinda sorry you got caught,

Miss Mary. Then again, if you'd got away, Bill woulda killed me for sure. So it ain't *all* bad news I guess."

"You have kind eyes, Squirrel Prewitt," I said, and he looked away, like he was embarrassed at receiving a compliment. "What's going to happen, Squirrel? Why am I here?"

"Keep your voice down," he said, so quiet it was lower than a whisper. "They left messages for your Pa. They reckon he'll bring your Town Marshal, and swap himself over for you."

"Oh. But your brothers want to *hurt* Father, don't they?"

"Yes, Miss. Not just them, but..."

He heard a noise just outside, and his head turned sharply toward the door, but no one came in. He put a finger to his lips to remind me to keep quiet, then went on, whispering into my ear from just inches away.

"We can't change this, Miss Mary. Not the part about the revenge and your Pa. But when he comes, it's my job to make sure *you* don't get too far."

"But—"

"Quiet, we don't have much time. Now don't cry out or nothin', Miss Mary, just listen. Cause I promise I ain't gonna do what they told me to do. Promise not to cry out?"

I inched my face toward his and nodded, didn't speak.

"Alright. They told me to shoot the Town Marshal, and I said I just couldn't. Especially not now I've met him. I never shot no one before, not even a stranger. So anyways, Henry belted me one, and said to just shoot your horses then, once you're three or four miles away. Before you get to where any people are, is the reason."

"But you wouldn't do that, would you, Squirrel? You wouldn't shoot my lovely pony." I looked in his eyes as I waited for his answer, and time seemed to slow down too slow, and my heartbeat was the loudest sound in the room.

"No, a'course not," Squirrel half-whispered. And his kind eyes were telling the truth. "I wouldn't shoot *any* horse, ever. But listen up, this is important — you gotta tell Town Marshal Rollins to help me. I think it'll all be okay if he helps me. I believe in your Pa, Miss Mary, there's a rightness about him. He'll fix this, and I reckon I know how to help him to do so. Tell Town Marshal Rollins, okay?"

"Alright, but—"

"If I get killed, Miss Mary, you tell your Pa this from me — I know he was right, that I need to do my own thinking. That's why I done what I done. And I just hope I thunk the right thoughts when I worked it all out."

Heavy footsteps were coming, Squirrel looked to the door as it opened — and I closed my eyes and pretended I was sleep.

CHAPTER 27
THE POSSE

Me and Georgina and Rollins were coming up to a part of the trail that worried me. I had been this way only once before, and while the trail was wide enough for a small wagon, it was thickly treed on both sides. I was worried about Prewitts — if they wanted to ambush us, this would be a good place. And too, it was the last bushy area before we would come to the Monte Vista Road.

Me and Sam Rollins rode with our rifles at the ready, and in a strange moment, we looked at each other and stopped.

We'd both thought it at once.

"I should drop back now," he said, "and follow at a distance, here on."

I nodded a slow, respectful one at him. I almost gave him some suggestions, but knew then, he didn't need them. Just like his mother, Sam Rollins was more than he seemed. He was fully committed to this now, whatever it took.

He wished us good luck, stepped down off his horse, and waited in some shade there as we rode away.

Georgina was completely unarmed — my decision. She'd a'been more chance of shooting me or Mary than of shooting a Prewitt. I think she was secretly relieved when I told her she wouldn't be touching no guns today.

"I'll teach you and Mary to shoot tomorrow," I now told her. "Won't need much help today. I been through worse situations, up against better men and worse skunks."

Hard to sound like I really believed it, but I done my best.

Her only reply was a nod — a nod of trust, love, and hope. That was all she could manage, but it was enough. We would do what we could, and face this together, like always.

If we had to lie and pretend in order to get through this, then that's what we'd do — the real truth was in what we felt for each other, and even my death would not change that.

My life for theirs — a fair trade if I had to make it. But I weren't about to just lay down and die, I'd be taking some Prewitt skunks with me, whatever that took. My girls would be safe when this ended.

Silently we rode the narrow trail through the forest, then the trees thinned both sides as we neared the Monte Vista Road.

And there they were right in front of us — not the Prewitts, but half of the posse. Sheriff Sullivan Simms was off his horse, looking at the ground, like as if he was tracking.

I didn't look at Georgina, but I sure heard her thinking. She didn't say nothing, a'course, she's too clever for that.

Luke Golden sat his horse, watching Simms — as did the other man, the hard case who'd looked so pleased with himself in Los Angeles, earlier today. He wore six-guns on both of his hips, and a Winchester in a scabbard on his back, just as he had in town.

It weren't looking good. And I knew I would not get a chance to speak to Luke Golden in private.

Shoulda planned a diversion.

Rusty, I am.

Too late now, they already seen us.

"Hail the posse," I called. "Two of us approaching. Are your other three members nearby? If so, call them off."

Deputy Luke Golden called, "Frakes," and waved us on in before calling out, "Just us three here."

"Keep behind me," I told my wife, "and let me do the talking. I'll get Golden alone if I can, but don't try to help, Simms'll notice."

As we got close, it was Simms who spoke to us. "Changed your mind did you, Frakes? Got brave and come to join us now." Then, seeing that it was Georgina riding behind me, he added, "What's *she* doin' here?"

I didn't reply, only watched him, read him by his eyes and his movements. *Almost sure he's a wrong'un[1]. But almost ain't sure.*

"What's happened, Mister Frakes?" said Luke Golden. "You could not have known we'd be here. Something terrible's happened." His eyes showed concern, but his voice stayed sharp and clear like a good lawman's should.

"It's Mary," I answered. "The damn Prewitts took her. They left notes that led me to here. Where's your other three posse members?"

"You ain't the only one who can track, Frakes," said Simms. "The Prewitts split into two groups, so we sent the other three after the man who went west. They was all useless anyway — bit like yourself these days, Frakes."

"Sheriff Simms, please," said Deputy Golden. "We need to put personal differences aside, and all work *together*. Those we're tracking now kept going west, did they not?"

"Any fool can see that," growled the hard case. "Look at all the damn tracks, they might's well have painted a sign with a big red arrow writ on it. Let's move, we got killin' to do." His eyes were on me when he said the last bit, and he seemed almost amused. Still, I could not be certain of anything. Right now, there was nothing I could do — this all had to play out somehow, now we were in it.

"I'm Lyle Frakes," I said to him, wiping my right hand on my britches then offering it to him to shake.

"Frank. Frank S*mith,*" he growled, making a point of not shaking my hand. Instead, the skunk spat tobacco juice onto the ground near Horse's front feet.

"Easy now, feller," I said to my agitated animal. But the way I stroked his neck meant, *'You can bite the spittin' skunk later.'*

"Did they kill Town Marshal Rollins?" said Golden. "You told me he was watching over Mary today, so I wondered. And the schoolteacher too?"

"They're fine, they're *all* fine," Georgina said urgently. "Please, let's go and find Mary, we can talk on the way."

"No blood was spilled," I told Deputy Luke, as Simms mounted his horse so we could get going. "They tricked that fool Rollins and lied to the teacher, left a note for me to come. We can make a plan as we ride. But I'll tell you now, we ain't risking Mary's life by starting up something before she's clear of the dance floor."

Simms, with the hard case beside him, took the lead at a trot, while me and Golden rode side-by-side right behind them, with Georgina bringing up the rear.

As we rode, I explained to them all what my plan was. I would take Mary's place, take my chances inside, while Georgina and Mary rode for the safety of Los Angeles. And now the posse was here, they would sneak in on foot and surround the place — once we found it.

We were coming to the end of the wagon road, and there were tracks heading off in three different directions.

"Looks like you're expected," said Sheriff Sullivan Simms, wheeling his horse around something, then pointing at the ground there between us. It was an arrow made from tree bark, with the letter F beside it, made from small stones.

"Fine tracking, Simms," said Frank the hard case, with a laugh. "Can you shoot that good too?"

He knew. When he said what he said about arrows before, he knew that was going to be here. Some fools just can't help 'emselves.

A few minutes later I slowed some, got a few extra yards between us and the two men in front. "I'm glad *you're* here, young Luke," I said, quiet and meaningful-like. And with my eyes I tried to let him know I didn't trust Sheriff Simms or *'Frank Smith'* — did not trust them a half-damn-inch further than I could throw 'em.

"You alright, Frakes?" said Golden. "Something wrong with your—?"

"Tired is all," I said, and I rubbed an eye with one hand as Simms turned sharply toward us and stopped.

"What are you sayin' back there, Frakes?"

I couldn't start anything up without Luke Golden's help — and I had to say *something.* "We're agreed on the plan then? I go in alone, then soon as my girls ride away, you fellers unleash hell on the Prewitts, while I do whatever I can from inside."

That first arrow weren't the only sign they left for us. Twice more, the trail came to a fork, and both times they'd left me clear arrows. Once I thought I heard someone a short ways behind us — it could have been Prewitts, but it might too be Rollins.

It took every bit of strength I had in me to *not* turn around then — Rollins was *somewhere* back there.

If he could somehow find Golden when they all split up — but then again, *would they* split up as I'd planned it? And if they *did*, what would happen to Golden?

I feared for Luke Golden's life, but what could I do? He was good at his job, I knew that much, I just had to trust him. Perhaps he'd worked it out.

If he hasn't, he'll have to think mighty quick when the time comes.

And right then, perhaps almost a mile away, came three

rifle shots, a familiar pattern. *Bang ... then a five second pause ... then bang-bang.*

Deputy Luke Golden looked at me, raised his eyebrows. "That's the pattern of shots you've heard several times, Mister Frakes?"

"We must be close now," I said with a nod. "You boys should hang back, we can't have you seen by no Prewitts. Me and Georgina will go on without you. And good luck to each good man here."

---

1. WRONG'UN: Either a bad man, or someone who ain't quite right in the head. Often a wrong'un is both of these things.

CHAPTER 28
THE EXCHANGE

The world pushed in on us as we rode away from the others — all these damned orange trees, formerly fruitful, now endlessly clawing at the sky, no more life for them, evermore. Even now, with the streams all a'running, nothing would ever bring these trees back to life.

Stop it, Lyle, dammit.

I'd never have let all that get to me when I was younger.

I touched Horse's powerful neck as I rode, and took strength from his example. He ain't bothered by gloomful possibilities, and neither should I be. We're old, not useless, unless we give in to such feelings.

I got my mind back where it should be, told Georgina what she must do when she rides away with Mary.

"Instead of going to Los Angeles, you'll double back after a mile and skirt back around. Go to the big Spanish ranch house, top a'the mountain. You'll be safe there, whatever happens, while I take care of business. There's paths all through the forest, just keeping going uphill and you'll get there."

She studied my face before saying, "He's a Prewitt, isn't he? That Frank? He knew the arrows would be there."

I stared at her, astounded. "You woulda made a fine sorta lawman, Princess. Anything else you think I mighta missed?"

"I love you, Kit."

"You thought I mighta missed that?"

"No." She smiled a beautiful one and said, "I needed to say it, that's all. For my own reassurance."

We stopped a moment, right there, just looked into each other. We both knew the truth — this might be the last time. *But then, ain't that always the truth?*

I didn't need words to tell her what she already knew.

A few seconds later, another three a'them shots.

Bang … then a pause … then bang-bang.

Half-mile ahead.

"We'd best go," she said. "Mary's waiting. Thank you, Kit. For everything you do, what you've always done. It'll be okay, won't it?"

"I won't let you down, or her, or myself. We got things to look forward to. And besides, who'd look after this ornery horse if I weren't around?"

We rode along the trail in silence the rest of the way, and soon enough came to the place. A small stream ran through it, and the foot-long grasses swayed as a light breeze rose up from behind us.

Pretty little place. I bet Mary thought so when she spied it.

And the grass was beaten down plenty in a path to the house, and round the back of it too. They had been here maybe two weeks — *I shoulda gone lookin'.*

"He's here," a loud voice called out from the porch of the little clapboard cabin on the side of the hill.

A rifle shot rang out from the trees further off to our left, then another from the right.

"Don't worry," I said as Georgina startled. "That's just to let us know they got us in their sights, so's we see the good sense in behaving. One ain't even in range, less he's got a Sharps in there with him as well as that Winchester. But they don't plan to shoot us today, or they would have already."

As we rode farther into the clearing, a second hard case came out onto the porch and called out, "Who's that with you, Frakes? It ain't round enough to be Rollins."

"It's my wife," I called back. "I don't trust the lawmen round here."

"We got that in common," he called, which was followed by laughter. "You best put that rifle down now, and we'll meet in the middle with the girl."

"You know that ain't how it works," I called back. Horse was still moving forward, but he was itchy to start something up. Prancing like a Spanish show pony he was, head on his chest and muscles all coiled, and I had to keep him under tight rein. "Rifle stays in my hands til they've ridden well out of our view. After that, I lay it down and come along quietly."

"Always worth a try."

The two men went to opposite ends of the porch, their

rifles pointed at me as someone else came through the doorway.

It was Mary in front, then the Prewitt girl.

Our *new friend,* Eliza.

We were halfway into the clearing.

Far enough.

I drew rein and we stopped right there.

"Stay on your horse, Princess," I said. "We'll wait for them here. And no matter how much you want to, don't do *anything* when they bring her. And don't lose your temper, not even with words."

"Alright, Kit."

"You too, Horse. Behave now, I mean it."

I stroked the neck of my animal to calm him. Then I stepped down, still holding Gertrude. I stood beside Horse as they came — he was alert, but well-behaved for the moment.

One of the men from the porch disappeared behind the cabin a few moments and came back leading Dewdrop. She was saddled and ready to go, and she called to Horse when she seen him, but he didn't reply.

Arrogant sometimes, ol' Horse.

Eliza Prewitt took Dewdrop's reins from her bearded skunk brother, and she and Mary started the long walk toward us. The man picked up his rifle and came along too, ten yards from Eliza and Mary, off to their right, his spurs all a'jingle.

It surprised me that the Prewitt girl was unarmed — but then, it might likely ensure things went calmer. *Clever, now I thought on it.*

Anyway, the men was all armed aplenty, and them being spread out all around me, the girl's lack of a gun made no difference.

I wondered where Sheriff Sullivan Simms was, the skunk. And Frank Prewitt, and Luke Golden too.

And Rollins.

I got a lot riding on young Samuel Rollins. Shoulda brung John Williamson too. Too late now, Lyle, you rusty dang fool.

That ain't helping, Lyle. Enough!

Keep your mind right HERE where you're at.

"Where's the others?" I shouted. "I'd see you all here in my sight 'fore we do this."

There was no immediate answer, and I knew they could not comply — Frank Prewitt was with Simms and Golden.

Eliza said something to the bearded skunk who was escorting her, and after a quick discussion he called out. "Squirrel and Mike, both come forward where he can see you."

"One short, ain't you, Prewitt?"

"You know it, Frakes," he spat back. "The one with the Sharps aimed right at your head, in case you brought company and this is an ambush. We ain't stupid you know."

"If you say so," I called back, as the two fellers came into the clearing, one on each side. Squirrel's arm came up like as if he was going to wave to me — then he changed his mind and just stood there, trying to look outlaw-like with his rifle.

If only. If only...

I turned my attention back to the group who were walking toward us. They were still fifty yards away when Mary spoke — and a'course, she was still running her mouth when they got as close as they were coming, ten yards away.

"Father, Mother, it's *so* good to see you. What an adventure, don't you think? This is my new friend Eliza, please don't hurt her, Father, when you kill her brothers! And not Squirrel either, he's really quite lovely, you know, I think you were right about him. And look, Miss Eliza, do you see Father's wonderful horse? He's called Pale-Eye Champion Blaze, although *Father* just calls him Horse, which is *quite* unsatisfactory, but I guess you can't teach an old dog new tricks, as they say."

"Stop now, Mary," said Eliza Prewitt then, and put a hand on my daughter's arm — just light, how a friend would — and to my surprise, Mary stopped right there and then. Not just her talking, but also her walking.

"Mary, dear Mary," said Georgina. "They didn't hurt you, did they?"

"Well, no, although that mean ugly Henry wanted to tie me up and whip—"

"This one Henry?" I said, eyeing the rifle-pointing skunk who now stood just twenty yards away.

"No, I don't know this one's name, but I don't think— "

"Enough now, child," I said. "We'll discuss all that later, when I come home."

Eliza Prewitt ever-so-briefly half-smiled when I said that — a quizzical puzzlement, that smile, wrapped up in a riddle, or however they call it. Weren't normal anyway. Nothing about all this was.

"Mary dear," the Prewitt girl said, kind and sweet as you like. "It's been lovely to meet you, and I hope we might meet up again, under better circumstances sometime. But it's time you left now, my brothers need to speak with your father. And don't forget, Mary — *we're modern girls.* Now climb up on Dewdrop."

Mary smiled at Eliza and done as she'd been told to, then rode her horse forward to us.

I reached up and touched her dear face, told her, "Go with your mother now, good girl."

With one final look of goodbye, Georgina turned her horse about and my girls trotted their horses away as I watched. No shots were fired, no birds took to flight from the trees — no signs of problems at all.

As they reached the limits of my sight, they stopped, turned around, and they waved.

And then they were gone.

I stood a half-minute in silence, before Eliza Prewitt spoke from that same ten-yard distance behind me.

"Shall we go inside, Mister Frakes? I believe we have business."

CHAPTER 29
MARY, GEORGINA, ROLLINS & SQUIRREL

As soon as we rode out of Father's sight, I told Mother not to be afraid of whatever might happen. She asked what I meant, and I told her — "Squirrel has been told to chase us, and to kill Town Marshal Rollins, or at least shoot our horses so we have to walk."

"But Mary—"

"It's quite alright, Mother, Squirrel won't do it, he promised."

"But how does he know Rollins is here?"

"He doesn't," I said, as Dewdrop sped up to a nice easy canter. "You're here instead, of course. Sorry, I should have explained that, they thought it'd be the Marshal, rather than you."

"*Very* reassuring," she said. "Your Father told me to turn left after a mile, then go up the mountain."

We had been riding almost two minutes when the first shots were fired.

"I hope that's Squirrel," I said.

"No more talk, Mary, let's *go!*"

We rode *hell-for-leather,* as it's called in Father's dime novels. Fast anyway, as we weaved through the trees, ducking branches and we even jumped a small creek — it was such rollicking *fun!*

There were shots every ten seconds or so, but after a minute they stopped. Six shots, I'm certain.

"He's run out of bullets," said Mother, as we stopped at a fork in the trail. "Let's go left here."

"Mother, really? He's not out of bullets, that wasn't a six-gun, it was a rifle. Winchester if I'm not mistaken. Can you *really* not tell the difference?"

She didn't answer, she only said, "Quiet. Do you hear anything?"

Well, of course I heard *some* things. There was wind through the trees, and flies buzzing nearby, and now I listened properly, *yes, someone riding toward us!*

"Let's go," Mother said, and she motioned for me to go in front, for the trail she'd chosen was narrow. "Now, Mary!"

"We should wait here for Squirrel," I said. "But then, without Town Marshal Rollins, he won't know what to—"

"Mary, now!" she said more urgently, and I heard a *slap,* and dear Dewdrop took off along the trail.

"Don't *hit* her," I called over my shoulder. "That's the second time she's been hit today!"

We did our best on that trail, but the rider behind was getting closer. And there was another rider off to our left, and that's when I got confused.

Then as we came to a clearing, to my surprise, I heard the voice of Town Marshal Rollins. "Mrs Frakes, head on up that hill, I'll wait for him here!"

"Let's go, Mary," she cried, and took off at a gallop.

Then I saw what surely would happen — Town Marshal Rollins was going to kill Squirrel.

Well, I simply could not allow it.

I turned Dewdrop about, and rode toward where the Marshal had just jumped from his horse, and was pulling out his rifle from its scabbard.

"No, don't hurt him," I shouted from Dewrop's back. "Ride away, Squirrel, quickly!"

"Mary, get out of the way," the Town Marshal shouted, as he tried to see past Dewdrop and me.

I could hear Squirrel still on his way through the trees, he'd not heard my warning!

I hadn't been able to stop Dewdrop in time, and we'd gone right past Marshal Rollins. He was down on one knee now, taking aim at the spot where dear Squirrel would soon ride into the clearing.

"No, Marshal, don't shoot him," I called, as Mother came riding back toward us, yelling, "No, Mary!"

I jumped down from Dewdrop, ran at the Marshal as Squirrel rode into the clearing.

"MARY, NO," they all seemed to be yelling at once.

And as Town Marshal Rollins turned away from me, aimed up at Squirrel and squeezed the trigger, I leaped through the air — *like a tiger,* I thought at the time, *but as graceful as any fine dancer* — and slammed into Town Marshal Rollins as he fired the bullet.

But too late, too late, I saw, as dear Squirrel crashed to the ground. His horse skidded along, then jumped up and ran, ran for its life, leaving Squirrel behind.

And as Mother jumped off her horse screaming, and ran, ran toward me — dear Squirrel lay alone in the dirt. He was face down, not moving a muscle.

"Oh, Squirrel. No."

CHAPTER 30
"IF YOU SKUNKS HURT MY GIRLS..."

Once my girls rode away, I laid Gertrude down on the grass and led Horse away several steps, so the girl could pick Gertrude up, completely unhindered.

Her brother said somethin' then, in an attempt to sound mean, but it was just empty words. I ignored him, kept my upper story for thinking. My own mistakes had led me to here — I couldn't afford no more of 'em, if I wished to see my family ever again.

Such situations, most men make mistakes by letting their hatred get control of their minds. And while I weren't on friendly terms with these Prewitts, I didn't waste energy hating them. Plenty of time for that later, if you're that way inclined.

We walked to the house, and I watched for an opening, a'course. But they weren't complete fools.

Only good thing, they let me tie my own Horse to the porch rail. I tied him all the way at the end, well away from the door, where they hopefully would not notice the *way* that I'd tied him — he'd easy break loose if I called him, or if there was gunfire.

But that was the only thing that went in my favor.

Men with guns on me everywhere — and when I went through the door, one with a pistol, other side a'the room. Looked keen to use it, that feller, so I kept behaving while the others came in.

They didn't make no mistakes when they tied me up neither. The girl told them not to, but one grunted, "Boss's orders," and she didn't argue. They used a good four-strand grass rope to bind up my hands behind my back — there wouldn't be no workin' that loose.

Tie a bull to a fence, rope like that, and the fence will break 'fore the rope does.

Next they tied me to a chair, which they placed back near the far wall, right across from the door we came in by.

There was the girl and three brothers in with me. I knew that left three more Prewitt skunks out there somewhere — almost certainly, one of 'em was Frank. That left just two to worry on.

And one a' them two was Squirrel.

But what of the other?

Made me mighty nervous, that did. And then I heard a shot.

I looked at the girl, she just smiled. Not evil, just an ordinary smile.

"If you skunks hurt my girls—"

"It's just Squirrel," she said. "Steering them away from Los Angeles. No one will harm them, I promise."

Another shot.

"Why am I here? Why did you not just kill me, you filthy damn Prewitts?"

"I need a drink," an ugly bearded skunk growled.

"Go ahead," said another who looked no different to him. "If you want your throat cut so bad, be my guest. You know he told us to wait."

Another shot in the distance.

I looked at the girl, a few feet to my left, and she just sorta smiled. She was watching the door.

"Get on in there," came a rough voice from outside, and every face turned to the door, every gun pointed.

Every gun except Gertrude, that is. She was on the front porch, a few feet away from that door.

They musta got Rollins, I thought. *I know it ain't my girls, they'd be makin' some plentiful noise.*

"Brung you all a present," the voice called, as the first heavy boots clomped up the steps, followed by others. Then the same voice growled, "Open the damn door and get in."

The door swung open, and there was U.S. Deputy Marshal Luke Golden, with his hands held high in the air. No one said a word as he stepped inside, followed by that damn Sheriff Simms and Frank Prewitt, with their guns pointed at Golden's back.

"Hello, Frakes," Golden said. "Good to see you."

Then Eliza Prewitt took off, leaped at Golden from halfway across the room.

And he caught her in his arms and he kissed her — and they all started laughing.

CHAPTER 31
MARY LAYS DOWN THE LAW

"You've killed him, Marshal Rollins," I cried. "You've killed my dear Squirrel."

"Mary," Mother gasped. She was running toward me. "Mary, are you alright, child? Oh, Mary, you foolish girl, what were you thinking, you could have been killed!"

"Don't you move a dang muscle, young Prewitt," said Rollins, aiming his rifle at Squirrel's unmoving body again. "I'm wise to your tricks, stand up slow, and don't reach for no guns."

"Oh, you silly man," I told him, as Mother wrapped me up in her arms so I barely could breathe. "He's dead, can't you see? Squirrel wanted to *help* us, and look what you've gone and done!"

"Don't you believe it, young Mary, I've seen him play possum for a good twenty minutes after your father shot him. Besides which, I'm pretty certain I missed him, his horse fell, is all."

I could hear the horse running uphill in a panic, but when I watched Squirrel a moment, I saw he was breathing. I broke away from Mother's tight grip then, and ran over to Squirrel as both grownups yelled, "Mary, no!"

He was heavier than he looked, but I managed to roll him onto his back just as Mother arrived. Squirrel's face was covered in mud, and he looked quite peacefully asleep. Although strangely, he wore half a smile — the left side of him smiled, not the right.

"Keep the gun on him, Sam," Mother said, "just in case. But I think perhaps Mary was right — his rifle had been put away in the scabbard, I saw it as the horse ran away." Then gripping my forearm she said, "Oh, Mary, he's waking."

"Boss," he yelled with alarm as he opened his eyes. And then, "Mary, where's Town Marshal Rollins?"

The wonderful news was, Squirrel hadn't been shot at all. His horse had been jumping a log when it saw Samuel Rollins, and must have shied at the gun. *Well, wouldn't you?* The poor thing had attempted to turn in mid-air, lost its footing on landing and fell, then skated along in the leaf litter — losing its lovely rider — before jumping up and running away, helter-skelter.

"Dang spook of a horse," Squirrel said. "I never have no luck with horses. One day I'll have a horse a'my own, and train him to trust me."

"That horse saved your life," said the Town Marshal from a few feet away, his rifle still pointed as he stopped. "You were square in my sights when I started to squeeze at the trigger. Now, no sudden movements, young Squirrel. You got fifteen seconds to explain yourself."

Well, I do get cross when people don't listen!

"I told you why he's here *already*," I cried. "Squirrel's come here to help us, he told me he would! Put away that silly rifle right now, you're making him nervous, how *can* he talk with that horrible thing pointed at him?"

"It's alright, Miss Mary," said Squirrel. "I'm used to them rotten skunk brothers a'mine pointin' all sorts a'guns at my head. I ain't nervous at all, the Marshal here ain't gonna shoot me, I ain't done nothin' wrong. But I would like some water to get all this dirt out my mouth and my elsewheres." And he snuffled a little and brushed at an ear, as if to explain what *elsewheres* were.

Speaks as strangely as Father, this Squirrel.

"Mary, bring him some water," said Mother, "while I check his pockets for weapons, just to be certain."

Squirrel sat on his rear with his knees bent, his hands in the air, and wearing a smile, while I went for the water. He *did* look a sight, with his mischievous grin and white teeth, and shining blue eyes in the midst of all that dark mud.

"He has no guns or knives," Mother said, as I handed Squirrel the canteen and my handkerchief, so he could clean himself up.

Of *course*, being a *boy*, he did not clean his face thoroughly. But a few seconds later he had cleared his mouth and nose of all muck — he now looked like a raccoon, all that dirt being still around his eyes — and then he spoke quickly and urgently.

"We gotta go back and save Mister Frakes, but we gotta wait for the right moment. You gotta trust me, Town Marshal Rollins. I know you think I'm no good, but Mister

Frakes says I *can* be a good man — so even though you can't trust me, you should trust *his* judgement, I reckon."

"And me," I said, gripping Samuel Rollins's arm. "I trust Squirrel too, just as Father does. *Please* do whatever he says. He just wants to help us save Father, and do the right thing."

The Marshal searched for something in my eyes, then in Squirrel's, and finally my Mother's. Then quietly, simply, he said, "Georgina?"

She never looked more lovely, my mother, as the wisdom shone out of her beautiful face, and a few errant strands of her silver hair bothered her eyes. And she smiled just a little as she said, "I've never quite understood why it is, that my husband sometimes trusts outlaws just as much as he trusts the best lawmen. He says this boy will become a good man, *if* he escapes from his brothers. And he's *here,* isn't he? *Away* from his brothers, not with them."

"So that's a yes, Ma'am?"

"I've always trusted Kit's judgement, Sam. And he's never let me down yet. So I guess my money's on Squirrel. Do whatever he says."

"You might not like what I tell you to do, Ma'am," said Squirrel. "And I *know* Mary won't."

"Tell us," said Mother.

"And hurry," said Samuel Rollins.

And Squirrel Prewitt was right — we did *not* like what he said. He said Mother and I must go somewhere else, while he and Town Marshal Rollins went back to save Father without us.

I argued of course.

But Mother placed her hand on my arm, looked into my eyes and said — very softly and wisely — "A deal's a deal."

And we stayed away from the action, bit our nails, and prayed for good news.

CHAPTER 32
ON A KNIFE'S EDGE

"Y ou shoulda seen the look on your face, Frakes," said Sullivan Simms. "I'm gonna commission a painting, so's I can enjoy it the rest of my days."

"Laugh it up, Simms," I said. "You'll be looking at your painting in a cell."

"Big talk for a dead man," he said, putting his six-gun back in its holster, but not tying it down.

"Get down now, Eliza," said Golden. She had been hanging off him a whole minute, and she kissed him again before sliding off him and half-smiling at me.

"Clever, Luke, ain't you?" I said. "I thought it was Simms."

There was still something odd here. Something...

"No problems in town, boss?" said the one they called Henry.

"All good," Golden answered, walking over to me. "Time for some fun now, boys, just as I promised. Don't you love it when a plan comes together? Let's have ourselves a drink and get started."

Two of 'em grabbed bottles and pulled out the stoppers, commenced to pour the contents down their throats — but Golden yelled, "Slow down, boys, that just ain't civilized, we got a guest here today. We'll drink out of glasses, like proper good people."

A half-minute later, all them fellers was drinking up whiskey — from tin cups, not glasses — like there weren't no tomorrow.

Throwin' 'em back one a minute, them big bearded fellers, to start with. Eliza, she just sipped at hers once — she screwed up her face, put the cup down, then sat back in a corner and watched.

Golden and Simms threw one down, grabbed a second, but I noticed that neither was drinking so fast as the Prewitts.

Five minutes in, Luke Golden walked over to me and said, "Drink, Frakes? You're going to need it."

And the Prewitt boys all laughed and cheered.

"Keep it," I told him. "I don't drink with skunks. You're a damn disgrace to the badge, that's what you—"

He threw the whiskey in my face, threw the cup against the wall, then punched me in the left ear, hard enough so it rang, and my dang chair fell over.

"You hit like a sad little girl," I said from the floor. But in truth, it hadn't been too bad a punch. He'd improved since our fight in Santa Monica.

"Pick him up," he said, grimacing, and rubbing at his

wrist — he had hurt it. Some fellers just never learn to punch right, or at least get it wrong when they're angry.

It felt good to know it hurt him too — sore hand went good with his still blackened eye, and I'd make sure he hurt worse than that before this was all over.

Two a'them ugly fellers put my chair upright, and set it up back against the wall so it wouldn't fall so easy next time.

Looks like they plan to enjoy this awhile, they surely ain't in no hurry.

Golden leaned down and stared into my eyes. "Why are we here, *Mister* Frakes?" Then over his shoulder he said, "I spilled my drink, boys, bring me another. And a bottle for our friend."

He had two a'them boys hold my head up, while he poured that bottle a'whiskey all over me — I *guess* he was tryin' to get it to go down my gullet, but to do it successful, he woulda needed to keep the bottle inside my mouth. A little went down, and soon I was coughing and spluttering fit to drown as some went down the wrong hole — but when that bottle was empty, there weren't much inside me. Most of it soaked into my clothes, with a little on Golden's.

Almost like he just done it for show.

"Drink up, boys," he said then. "You've earned it. It's time for our guest to hear a story, now he's had a nice drink."

"That's some fine hospitality, Luke," said Sullivan Simms, and the Prewitt boys laughed and drank up, while Eliza sat back and half-smiled.

That strange little half-smile.

Golden dragged a chair over to mine now. "Do you know why we're here, Frakes? Can't hazard a guess?"

"Because these Prewitts' damn cousins tried to kill me, and got what they asked for?"

"Let me hit him now," growled the one they called Joe.

"Not his head," said young Golden, smiling, and leaned outta the way to give Joe some room.

He was a biggun, Joe Prewitt, and likely knew how to punch. But for a first thing, there was already five bottles empty, and he'd drunk more than his share — and for a second thing, I was sitting down low on a chair, with my belly not much above his knee height. He gave it his best, but it was no pile-driver — more a pile a'dung, that punch he drove into my belly.

"One more," he yelled, but Golden told him to come back when he'd finished his bottle.

"I'm gonna tell you a story, Frakes," said Luke Golden, his look now intense. "My father fought in the war and survived it somehow. Came home to burned land, a sick wife, and no way to feed us. I had three older brothers — fifteen and sixteen they were, two of them were twins. They all died in that war. I was too young to go, of course. I was eight when it ended, and my father came home."

"Terrible thing, war," I said. I don't think he heard me.

"My father did some things wrong. To *survive*, that was all. He was a *good* man. He didn't kill anyone, but he stole in order to feed us."

"Many did."

He went quiet a moment, looked right through me to

some other place, then suddenly blinked himself back to the room. "You don't even remember him, do you, Frakes?"

And his whole face turned into a snarl.

I looked into Luke Golden's eyes, looked into his face, looked into his hatred. And there — some in the eyes and some in the face, but mostly there in the hatred — I saw his father.

"Bell," I said, soft and uncertain as I searched my memory. "No, it was Bellow. Dick Bellow, yes? Or no, maybe not quite."

"Richard," said Golden. "Richard Bellow."

"Rick, he went by," I said. "I remember him, Luke, *and* your mother. I remember *you* too. All arms and legs and good manners, with neat slicked back hair like your Pa. And you had the same name as he did, except for they called you Ricky."

"Ricky," he murmured, like as if he had never heard the word, and did not know its meaning. But the soft eyes hardened again, and he added, "Been awhile since I heard it. No one left alive to call me that now."

"I'm sorry," I said. "Your mother was a—"

"Don't you *ever* speak of my mother," he growled, and he winced as he clenched his fists.

The drinking had gone on around us, and right then Frank Prewitt intruded on our conversation. "My turn to hit thish damn schkunk," he said, lurching toward me, and loading his fist as he did so. "Thish one fer my cousin Billy!"

But as Frank let the wild punch fly, Luke Golden leaped

out of his chair, deflected Frank's arm with his own, and spun him about as he whipped out a knife, so fast my eyes couldn't keep up. Blade was pressed to Frank's throat 'fore he knew it, and both men's eyes was now wild for different reasons.

"Boss, please," Frank said into the sudden stillness and silence, as all eyes watched that thin, deadly blade.

"Just joshing you, Frank," Golden said, but the laugh that came out of him sounded completely deranged, as he let Frank go free. "Just don't hit our *guest* in the face, Frank. I want him still conscious when I start to *burn* him, and to watch while I slice off the cooked bits."

"Sure, boss," said Frank, still uncertain, as he eyed the thin blade. He backed away from Luke Golden, huffed out a breath as he rubbed at his throat, before turning toward me and smiling. But that smile was shaky.

"Not his head," Golden said once again.

Frank Prewitt bent low at the knees, drew back his fist and drove a straight right at my belly — but I reckon his heart weren't all in it, his mind still back where it had been ten seconds ago.

His action was good, but there weren't no power behind it.

Truth is, I been hit harder by Mary for callin' her doll Princess Mudbottom.

I almost felt bad for the poor Prewitt skunk. *Almost, maybe not quite.*

"Nice punch, Frank," Golden said though, and his blade was nowhere to be seen now. Then he piled new lies onto that one by saying, "That hurt the old coot but good.

Here, take my drink, Frank, you earned it. Your right hand's still King of the fists."

Seemed that was enough to restore all Frank's pride, and his brothers all cheered, drank a toast to his prowess as a fighter. Didn't stop after one toast, they drank a second to Luke Golden's jest, then a third to that skunk Sheriff Simms for the ongoing help he had pledged to the gang.

"We're gonna be rich, boys," Simms yelled, as they uncorked another two bottles.

As the ugly bearded ones done some more drinking — I noticed the lawmen themselves never actually drank much — young Deputy Luke went on with his sorrowful story.

Problem was, young Luke Golden had a mighty skewed view of the truth, when it came to that story.

Way he seen things, *I, Lyle dang Frakes,* was the one who'd done wrong — his whole life had been lived for revenge, and now I would pay.

CHAPTER 33
BILL BRYDEN, BRANDY & BURNS

P roblem with living your life for revenge, is the truth gets twisted up more in your mind every year. So by now, me and Luke saw that story as two different things.

And one just weren't true.

Simple truth of the story is this — about a year after the war, his father fell in with a bad bunch. They robbed a few stages and got away clean a few times. But one day it went wrong — as it always eventually does. The stage guard shot one of their gang, then another of their gang shot the guard.

Both men killed stone dead.

But instead a'riding away, that fool gang all stood round and argued about what to do — and though they were masked, the dang fools used each other's right names as they argued things out.

Thing was, one of 'em wanted to kill all the witnesses, and three of the others sort of agreed, more or less — it was only Rick Bellow who spoke out against it, and in the end he talked the others around.

That was the irony of it — if Deputy Luke Golden's father hadn't spared them four souls, he would not have been sentenced to jail just two weeks later.

If you ain't worked it out yet, it was me who arrested Rick Bellow — me and my partner, a wild sorta feller who was known as Shotgun Bill Bryden. Ol' Shotgun Bill had the consumption, but he reckoned no mere bloody cough was enough to kill *him* — his plan being to cure it by drowning it nightly in whiskey. Drank a whole lotta that potential cure he did, but anyone could see he was slowly losing the battle. He died six months later in a shootout outside Kansas City, saving my life in the process. But all Shotgun Bill ever wanted was to die with his boots on, so I guess it weren't *all* bad. We was Federal Deputy Marshals back then, same as young Luke Golden is now. Difference is, me and ol' Shotgun had honor, and respect for the job entrusted to us by the people.

Rick Bellow tried to bribe us when we caught him. Fair whack of cash it was too. Told us his whole sad story, even asked who would raise his poor son when he went to the hoosegow[1].

But just like ol' Shotgun told him, it was out of our hands. There was already a Warrant, and even if we let him go, someone else would find him in a day or two — and they'd maybe kill him as well. The man they had killed was the stage owner's brother, and he'd posted sizable bounties on their whole gang — dead or alive. And it was made clearly known, that *dead* was their preference.

Why, we had to fight two fellers off just to get Rick to town.

Two days later, I spoke for Rick Bellow at his trial, and reminded the judge what the witnesses said — that it was Rick who saved their lives, when the others was ready to murder 'em right where they stood.

"Takes a decent man to stand up for what's right," I said that day in court. "And he stood up to men who'd just killed. That takes stones, and demonstrates goodness of heart. Rick Bellow never killed no one, and it's clear how repentant he is. Got mixed up with this bad bunch is all, and I'd ask you go light on him, Judge."

Judge Forrest took all that into account, only gave him ten years, not twenty like most of the gang got. It was only the shooter himself who swung from the gallows — which was fair and right, what he done. That guard had a young family.

And so, here we were, twelve years later, me and his son in an old broken-down clapboard cabin.

And he holds all the Aces.

But that don't mean I ain't got no cards — I still got my brain and my voice, anything's worth a try, this situation.

"I done what I could, even gave your Ma money, Ricky."

This time it weren't the blade he pulled out, but his Colt — he was lightning fast, and he pushed it up under my chin, his eyes wild as he said, "Don't you call me that, Frakes, or I'll blow your damn head off right now."

"Luke," came the voice of Eliza then, soft and caring. "It's okay."

"Alright, girl," he said, without looking at her, and he holstered the six-gun again. Then looking into my eyes, he said, "That's the last time you mention my mother. You do it again, I'll visit your family later, you understand?"

"Luke, *no*," said Eliza, the shock of it plain in her voice.

I looked back at him, nodded agreement. No Ricky, no mother, those was our rules. *For the moment.*

"He died, Frakes, died in that jail. A man cut his throat."

"I'm sorry to—"

"No you ain't, it was *you* sent him there."

"Luke, I just did my job. I spoke for him at the trial, got his sentence reduced. You were there. You remember."

He looked away, looked at Eliza, breathed out a sigh, turned back to face me. "You coulda let him run. He had all that money from the stage, and he offered you half. You ruined our lives, and you got him killed, and it killed my poor mother. It's *you*, Frakes, who did this to him, and to her, and to me. And it's *you* who will pay. Oh, you'll *pay*, and you'll know how it feels."

Then he stood, turned away from me, faced all the Prewitts. They were strewn about the room now — two of them leaned in a corner, arguing something, so drunk their slurred words made no sense. Another was slumped in a chair, asleep with his head on the table, and the remaining two sat on the floor, their backs propped up against walls, each spilling more than they were drinking.

One a' them floor-sitters had puked on himself, and the place smelled worse than a saloon.

"Boys," Golden announced, "I just remembered, I bought you a bottle each of the best top-shelf brandy to celebrate." There was two sort-of-cheers and a groan before he went on. "Best of all, it's the brandy Frakes favors — so I'm gonna use my bottle for fuel to set him on fire with, won't that be good fun?"

Couple more half-hearted cheers from the Prewitts still standing, and one from the floor.

Golden then said, "Eliza, step outside and fetch my saddlebags, won't you? That's where I left the bottles."

"I got two nice bottles out there too," said Sullivan Simms. "I'll come help you, Eliza."

"Bandy," muttered Frank Prewitt from the floor. "Bing me ban ... brrr-randy. Brandy. Iss time a'kill Fakes." He picked up his cup, raised it up near his mouth and then dropped it. The tin cup rolled away as Eliza and Simms stepped out onto the porch, and Frank watched it, slack-jawed, unable to move, as it rolled out of his reach.

If Town Marshal Rollins is out there right now — if he's watching — I might yet have a chance — these Prewitts is all so drunk they can't pick their guns up, let alone aim them.

"You ever been burned, Frakes?"

"Burn Fakes," mumbled Frank, while the one they called Joe banged his cup against the wall a few times and said, "Burn." Then he fell over sideways, his bearded right cheek in the puke on the floor, and giggled to himself like a fool.

"No, Luke," I said after that. "I've never been burned, not proper. I been shot and stabbed, kicked and bitten by horses, including that unfaithful pale-eyed skunk just outside. But I never been burned, except spilling coffee on myself." Then I smiled right at him and added, "But who knows, young Luke — you never know if you like a thing til you try it."

"Oh, this is gonna be something," he said, his voice honed and tight and intense now, as his breathing slowed down. "You should enjoy this, Lyle Frakes." And I saw by his eyes, he was worked up and ready, ready to kill, and he'd follow this through to the end.

And still, no sign of Rollins.

Then the door opened up, and Simms stepped half-sideways into the room — just half a step really, a bottle showing in his left hand.

"Thanks for your help, skunks," said Luke Golden then, and he drew his six-gun and fired, and fired, and fired — and Sheriff Simms fired too, again and again.

They filled them drunk Prewitts with bullet after bullet, and soon there was no sound, no movement — them ugly bearded skunk Prewitts was dead, gone to Hell to meet up with their cousins.

Not one of 'em got to his gun. All murdered, cold blooded, by *lawmen*.

And I'd sat there and watched it, tied tight in my chair, waiting for my own bullet. I could taste my own death in the gunsmoke — yet no bullet came.

No bullet.

No bullet came.

And neither did Rollins.

1. HOOSEGOW: Jail. It comes from a Spanish word JUZGADO, which means Courthouse.

CHAPTER 34
LAMP OIL & GUNSMOKE

"L et's get outta this stinkin' damn smoke," said Sullivan Simms between coughs, and he walked out the door.

"Bring the horses, Simms, while I get this place ready to burn."

Not words I'd been hoping to hear.

"No sign of young Squirrel yet," Simms growled. "He shoulda been back by—"

Golden ignored him completely. "Get in here, Eliza," he called. "I want you to see what we've done. You'll be safe now, girl."

"I ... I can't," came her voice from outside, small and scared as a child's. "Don't make me look, Luke. Please don't."

"I told you, get in here right *now*. You don't have to *look,* just get in here, it's mostly smoke anyway. NOW!"

I didn't say anything. Perhaps he thought I was dead — I sure couldn't see him on the other side of the room.

No such luck.

"Enjoy that, Frakes, did you? Not exactly conventional law work, but it got the job done. Ah, here she is, my Eliza."

"Please don't make me—"

"Shut up," he snarled. "You don't have to look at your dear departed brothers, I just brought you in here for your safety. My opinion, the useless Town Marshal Rollins is out there somewhere — and I don't want you getting hurt when he tries to shoot Sheriff Simms."

"Oh," she said. "I ... I just wish..."

"Never mind what you wish, it's all done now. So, Mister Frakes, you've been quiet. But you'll answer me now, or I swear I'll go after your family when this is all done."

"Luke!"

"Shut up, Eliza," he said, but his tone wasn't mean, just impatient. "Tell me now, Frakes, is the stupid fat Marshal out there or not?"

"I hope so," I said. "But I doubt it. I made him wait for my girls, escort 'em to safety. Told him not to come back without the Spaniards from the ranch on the mountain."

That WOULD have been a good plan. My damn brain's gone to mush this past year.

With the smoke mostly cleared now, I watched Golden reload his six-gun as he spoke.

"Squirrel's not back yet," he said, smiling in that smug way of his. "I told him to chase your girls west, run them around until they get lost, then get himself back here. Always does what he's told, young Squirrel, and it's almost dark now. He'll be back any minute, unless your friend Rollins has killed him."

"No, not my dear brother, not—"

"I said shut up, Eliza, I won't tell you again."

I could not see her face, as she'd never turned round, not wanting to see her dead brothers — but when she spoke, she sounded more confused than alarmed. "Why are you being so mean, Luke? You told me we'd all be free, all be safe. Squirrel will come back, of course he will, won't he?"

"Yes, of course he will. It'll all be alright, girl."

Eliza grabbed hold of Luke now, clung onto him with her eyes closed as she pleaded for answers. "Luke? I don't understand. Why aren't you untying Mister Frakes, now the shooting's all over? You've done your job, killed the gang. You didn't *really* kill Squirrel's guard, did you? That was just a story for my brothers, wasn't it, Luke? Wasn't it?"

He unclamped her clawing hands from him as she started to sob, and she buried her head against the door in despair. Then Golden removed the lid from a large drum of lamp oil, and the smell of it spread through the room as he poured it while speaking.

"You wanna die in this building, Eliza Prewitt? Is that it? Would *you* like to burn? No? Then shut your damn mouth awhile. I told you it'll *all* be alright, and it will. Squirrel's fine, I changed the plan is all — and I never killed no one, we just paid the guard to leave town. So just shut your mouth, get outside and go help with the horses."

He poured *gallons* of lamp oil over the bodies; all through the room; on the drapes; on the dried out wood of the tables and chairs; on every last thing that would burn.

"You're good, Luke," I said after she left us, as he went right on pouring. "She still believes you. And sending Simms out there alone, knowing that Rollins would shoot him if he was there. What a fine brain you have. You coulda become a great lawman, son."

"I'm not your damn *son!*" He was mighty on edge now.

Time to turn up the heat.

"Must be turning in her grave, that fine woman you used to call Mother."

"Don't you mention *my mother* again, or so help me, I'll—"

Simms called to Golden from outside then. "Horses are ready, Luke. You right to go?"

"Get in here and untie Frakes from the chair. We're taking him with us."

I watched through the doorway as Simms handed over the reins of three horses to Eliza, then clomped up the stairs and came in.

Sheriff Sullivan Simms looked around at the Prewitts dead bodies, all riddled with bullets. Place smelled like whiskey and brandy, lamp oil and gunsmoke.

"Change of plan, Luke?" he said as he untied me from the chair.

But Golden only said, "Frakes isn't getting out of this quickly. He'll learn what true suffering is, the way he deserves to. It just won't be here."

My hands were still tied behind my back — Golden held his Colt to my head while Simms untied my hands, then retied them in front of me so I could ride.

Same strong piece a' rope, and a real good knot.

Golden took a quick look outside, while Simms watched me, quietly gloating.

"Where's his damn horse?" said Golden from the doorway. "Frakes's horse, Simms, where is it?"

"I ... it was here before we killed the Prewitts. Guess it musta got scared and run off."

"Dislikes gunshots nearby," I said. "Same as his owner. He'll come when I call."

"Well we ain't got all day," said Simms, and I stuck my head through the doorway and called out, "Horse, come."

Ol' Horse came through the trees to our left, stopped and watched us a moment, before cantering closer, then stopping again twenty yards off. I soothed him with my voice, and he trotted on over, stood quiet but alert, not far from the other animals.

He was clever alright, young Luke Golden. He took no chances, walking inches behind me until we got to the horses.

If Rollins was out there somewhere — anywhere — he could not have got a clean shot without risk of killing me. Golden stayed between horses, watched on from there as Simms helped me up into my saddle.

Then Luke Golden took the reins of all the horses from the Sheriff, smiled a smug one and said, "Matches are in my left saddlebag. Go light it up, Simms."

CHAPTER 35
IRONY

Eliza Prewitt looked terrified. She shook as she sat her horse, looked like she'd be sick.

I don't know what Luke Golden told her, but it sure weren't the truth.

"My rifle," I said. "It's leaning up on the front wall there. Be a terrible waste, old campaigner like Gertrude. And ain't we too close to the house? Figured you'd want to watch, make sure it all burns."

"Frakes is right for once in his life," said Sullivan Simms. "The smell a'them bodies ain't somethin' I wish to be near to. I'll set the fire while you move away where it won't be so hot when you watch. Let's leave his gun there, watch it melt."

"Who's the boss here anyway, Simms?" Golden said. "Bring the rifle, I can make use of it."

Once again, Golden was clever — he tied all four horses together before we moved off. He weren't leaving me too much hope, that was certain and sure. And they'd tied my feet together, underneath Horse, with another good rope.

Only thing in my favor was, they'd not used the same rope for the horses that they'd used to tie me — it was only rawhide, and only a single strip of it. Horse could maybe get loose from the others if he tried hard enough. And if I went unwatched for a bit, I could saw at the rawhide with my rope, maybe weaken it some.

We moved away while Simms went back and moved Gertrude to a safe distance. As we walked our horses a good hundred yards down the field, Golden still walked between us — *he's still wondering if Rollins might be there. Well, I'm wondering too.*

Problem was, even if Rollins was waiting, the closest he could be was two-hundred yards off. At that distance, some men can shoot the eye out of a deer — but I doubted Rollins could shoot anywhere near that well. And he'd have to make two shots, not one — both Golden and Simms.

If he's here, he'll wait til we're nearer the trees. Down by the trail there, where I first came into this valley.

Me and Eliza turned in our saddles when we heard the sound. Simms had walked into the house, lit it up in a half-dozen places — and now he hightailed it out.

He could put in the licks when he had to — and the way that fire leapt up and took hold, he *sure* had to.

Took him a minute to scurry across to where we were — he picked Gertrude up on the way — and the noise of that fire, at first, drowned out all other noises.

By then, Eliza had turned the other direction, and when I looked, I saw she was sobbing. Guess she had mixed

TOUGH AS OLD BOOTS

feelings — they was terrible men, but they *were* her family, I guess. And it had been brutal and sudden. They had been murdered, when they shoulda stood trial, and been strung up for their misdeeds.

Then again, maybe she was just worried about Squirrel. I know I sure was.

We stayed awhile, watched it burn. Felt strange to think these might be my last minutes — these skunks weren't who I'd choose to spend 'em with. But that's just how it goes, I guess. You can't choose how it ends.

Then again, this weren't over yet.

There was no point going back to check if the bodies were burned. It had been thorough, alright. It dawned on me then, why he'd burned them. He'd go back when it cooled, shift things about, make it look like more bodies than it was — to account for Eliza not being there.

I don't know whether he loves her — hard to love anyone, maybe, when you're all filled up with bitterness, way Luke Golden is — but I know now, he truly does want to keep her.

And right there, that's a thing I can use.

"I figured it out, Luke," I said. "You burned it so you could say Eliza and Squirrel died in there too. Or is it just Eliza? Does Squirrel not matter?"

He laughed then, the orange of the fire making his eyes blaze, and he looked like a devil — a handsome one, but a devil. "You're good too, Frakes," he said. "And you got this one right. But there's things you're still missing. Oh, you'll enjoy it, I'm certain — not really *enjoy* it as such, but I'm sure you'll respect how much thinking it took, how much planning to make it all happen, to turn out just right."

"I doubt that somehow."

"He's still not here," said Eliza. "It's almost dark. We won't leave til he gets here, will we, Luke? I can't get on that train without him, I'd worry too much."

"I told Squirrel to meet us in town if he was delayed," Golden assured her. He still hadn't mounted his horse. He turned to Simms then and said, "Time we made tracks, Sheriff. I'll hold Frakes's rifle while you mount up. Gertrude, did you call her, Frakes? Never thought you'd be killed by your own rifle, did you?"

"That's called irony, Frakes," said Sullivan Simms, as he handed Gertrude to Golden, then stepped up into his saddle. "You'd know that if you weren't a fool."

Luke Golden's head turned toward me—

He smiled, actually winked—

Gertrude, there in his hands—

Death and smugness, there in his eyes—

Gertrude snapped into position—

Roared loud, how only she can—

Sheriff Sullivan Simms, so surprised—

His left hand reached up for his hat—

But his hat was gone—

And with it, the top of his head—

Simms slumped forward in death, slid down the neck of his horse to the ground as we watched in a terrible silence.

Then Eliza screamed once — just a short one, a squeak

more-or-less — then she too went quiet, but for her quick ragged breathing.

The horses had panicked at the gunshot, but the rawhide strip holding their bridles to each other's held firm. They could not go anywhere, and we settled 'em quick.

"You enjoy that one, Frakes?" said Luke Golden, as calm as you like. And he bent down to study Simms, his look fascination.

"And Mister Lyle damn Frakes," he added then, looking up at me, smug-smiling into my eyes. "Looks like *you're* up for murder. You killed Sheriff Sullivan Simms, as you threatened you would just this morning, right in front of a whole crowd of people. What a shame, what a terrible business. And what a disgrace."

CHAPTER 36
TWENTY YEARS

Eliza was muttering now, clearly distraught by how things had gone. One thing to listen to your evil skunk brothers gettin' shot to bits like they deserve to — another thing altogether to find out your man ain't right in the head, and has lied to you all the way through, beginning to end.

And worse, she might have lost Squirrel.

Golden ordered her to step down and give him a hand to load Sheriff Simms onto his horse.

I don't think the poor girl even heard him. Just muttered more, in her own world. Might be loco already, is my guess.

Luke Golden tried again to lift the dead weight of Simms to the saddle, and once again the horse moved, and Luke dropped the body a third time.

He looked at my tied hands, considered his options. I got my hopes up for a moment — but he's only evil, not stupid.

He said, "Frakes, position your horse against Simms' horse, so he can't back away." Then he added, "Or I'll do more than kiss your wife's hand, you better believe it."

I did what he said.

He managed to get Simms across the saddle this time. Then he lashed Simms to his horse, before attaching it to a lead rope.

He'd done all this before, by the looks — knew just how to rig it all anyway. And our three horses were still tied together, so none could go anywhere alone.

He picked Gertrude up off the ground then, pointed her at me a moment and laughed. "Don't worry, Frakes. You'll get a fair trial, and I'll even speak of your good character. I promise, old man, you won't swing." He took Simms' rifle out of its saddle scabbard, threw it away, and put Gertrude in its place. "The Judge will give you twenty years, Frakes — rest of your life in a jail, with some of the men you put in there. Won't *that* be fun?"

We started to ride, with Luke in the middle a'course. Just walking pace, it was quite dark now — the firelight behind us casting strange long shadows ahead of us. At least the breeze took the smell and the smoke away in the other direction.

"Maybe I *will* enjoy jail," I told him. "Yet to try it, but maybe I'll like it. And like I said before—"

"Shut up, Frakes, your turn to listen. My father suffered for years before dying in that hell-hole. *Your fault.* My mother never got over it."

"I had no—"

"We would have been fine if you'd just let him go *free!*

He was gonna go straight with the money from that job, move us further west and open a store. He told me that himself, the day of his trial! But you ruined it, Frakes. My parents are dead because of—"

"Oh, shut up, Ricky, you fool." I kept Horse plenty close, crowding Golden between me and Eliza, so he couldn't react too fast if he tried to.

"Don't you call *me* a fool, you—"

"Why not? What have I got to lose, Ricky Bellow? It's *your* damn turn to listen! It weren't me who robbed a stagecoach. That was your father done that. He knew the risk and he took it. And you've done this job, what, two years now? You know well as I do, outlaws never stop, *never*. Always one more dang job."

"He was a good—"

"Yes he was, your Pa *was* a good man, before he went wrong. And he always kept some a'that goodness, that's how I know it for sure. Even then at the robbery, he saved the lives of them innocent folk, and that's how he got caught. But look what you're doing *now*, Ricky. This don't bring no honor to your father — it only shames him. He'd tell you to stop, Ricky Bellow. Stop shaming your family right now!"

He had spun toward me as I spoke, our horses still walking slowly away from the fire — and the flickering orange of it glowed in his eyes and filled up our night.

He shook with rage then — *or was it shame too?* — and I knew he might just change his mind, shoot me right here and now.

But I knew too, the angrier I made him, the more chance I had. *Angrified[1] men make mistakes.*

And though properly tied, I sure wasn't helpless, not now I was with Horse — yes, I had a *real* horse under me, the best animal ever there was.

And Rollins, he still *might* be there, almost close enough now, in the trees, waiting for the right moment.

"Your mother too," I went on. "Fine woman, straight and true as they come. She wrote me, you know, thanked me for the money I sent."

"You didn't send her one penny! If you had, you would have remembered our name right away."

"I'm not a young man anymore. And a man can't remember every name of those he sent ... well, if you think I never helped no one else out, you can just go right on thinkin' it."

"You only sent money to stop yourself feeling so guilty. She told me you sent it, but I didn't believe her. You must have felt guilty to send it."

He was still between all our horses, I needed to draw him out from there, so Rollins could get a clean shot.

If Rollins is there...

"She had wrote to me, said you was troubled. Asked if I might come and speak to you, Ricky."

"She did not! And stop calling me that!"

"She did, Ricky Bellow, she did. I wrote back, told her it weren't a good idea. I'd seen how you looked at me, day of the trial. I told her she should move on, marry some nice city feller, let him gain your trust, see you right. Told her trust like that'd take time, and you'd never trust me anyhow."

"You were right about that, Mister Frakes. She was never actually married to my father, did you know that?"

He sounds like a child now.

"She told me that, Ricky."

"She married the local Town Marshal you know, when we moved to Black Rock, Colorado, to be near her cousins."

"That right, is it? I always meant to write her again, but you know how law work can get, I just never had time."

"His name was Jim Golden."

"And the Luke part?" I said, as we came ever closer to the trees at the end of the valley.

"Just thought it sounded honest," said Golden, and he sorta chuckled, a strange one, half-boyish, half-evil.

And right then, from a ways off ahead, came the sound of a young feller calling.

"Boss, is that you? It's just me, Squirrel, don't shoot me or nothin' like that. I got the job done."

---

1. ANGRIFIED: Made angry. (Like JV's wife gets when he tramps his muddy boots across her clean floor)

CHAPTER 37

"GUESS HE COULDN'T SHOOT WORTH A DAMN..."

"Squirrel," squealed Eliza. "Is that really you?"

The sound of his voice had brought her back from whatever dark place she had been in.

"Come on in," hollered Golden. And he sounded like himself again, not a child. "I knew you could do it, young Squirrel. I got our part done too." Then to me and Eliza, he said, "Stop now. Wait for him to come."

As we stopped Luke slipped out of his saddle, stood on firm ground, his hand resting on the butt of his six-gun. Between us, between all our horses, not my side of his own, but Eliza's.

He was good, this Luke Golden. Took no chances at all, even when things all went his way.

"Thought you coulda become a good man, Squirrel Prewitt," I called, as he came nearer to us. "Guess I was wrong, and you're just another damn Prewitt skunk."

"Oh, Squirrel," Eliza called again. "I thought you were dead."

"I told you it'd be fine," Luke smiled, not taking his eyes off the lone rider. "You should have more faith in me, girl."

Squirrel was just thirty yards away now, and he wheeled off to the side some as he slowed his mount to a walk. He looked at the horse Luke Golden was trailing, with Simms' lifeless body strewn over it, then stopped ten feet in front of us before speaking. Funny thing, he was off to one side a little, not in front of Golden as you might expect.

"Who's the dead man on the horse?" Squirrel asked. "Sheriff Simms, is it? I bet it was Frank who done got him. Holds his liquor better than most, Frank, I guessed he'd be trouble."

"Never mind that," Golden said. "What happened with you?"

"It was Mister Frakes' wife came for Mary, instead of Rollins. I chased 'em off like you said anyway. I was scarin' 'em off every which way, then suddenly, that Town Marshal Rollins popped up outta nowhere, started shootin' right at me."

"Guess he *couldn't* shoot worth a damn," I muttered.

And Squirrel said, "Reckon not. I had my rifle right there in my hands, and I just fired at him, never even aimed it I reckon. And danged if I didn't put one right through his chest. Well, I couldn't hardly believe it, but Rollins keeled right over, right there on the spot. Weren't my fault, boss, it just happened that way. Hey, how come Mister Frakes is tied up anyway?"

"Never mind that," the skunk Deputy said. "Well done, Squirrel, well done."

"Thanks, boss, I guess. It felt bad, you know, lookin' at him, all dead like that. Guess I never wanna do that again."

"And the woman and girl?"

"I went after 'em, boss, pretty quick. Fired some shots to flush 'em out, and I heard their horses take off. They never seen me kill Rollins. I'm glad about that, it feels bad enough already without—"

"So you ran them around on the mountain, just like I told you, until almost dark, so they'd stay away from us, be safe."

"Yes, boss. But I couldn't fire much, on account of leavin' my rifle behind back with Rollins, when I took his pistol. An accident, mind, I'd never leave my gun on purpose. Just look at this beautiful six-gun Rollins had though, I just *had* to keep it!"

And as Squirrel took out the gun, it was pointed at Luke Golden's chest — and Town Marshal Rollins called out from the trees, "You're under arrest for the murder of Sullivan Simms, put your hands in the air."

And Squirrel, he smiled a little, his finger on the trigger of that six-gun as he added, "He's right, boss, it's true. You really are under arrest."

CHAPTER 38
THE SWEETEST HORSE I
EVER KNEW

Young Squirrel and Rollins's hearts was in the right place — but the plan they had made would likely get us all killed.

Problem was, Luke Golden just weren't no ordinary man — he was gunfighter-fast. Quick as I've ever seen.

It was a suicide mission, to be standing where Squirrel stood now — just six feet from Luke Golden, but with his arm extended. And the six-gun shook in his hand.

Too close, Squirrel, too close.

Golden pulled on the reins of his horse with his left hand, and its head bumped Squirrel's arm sideways as Luke drew his pistol and fired.

He was dead to rights, Squirrel was in that moment — but Luke never counted on sisterly love. Eliza must somehow have sensed what would happen, and as Luke's gun came up to end Squirrel' s life, the girl leaped out of her saddle, landing on Luke as he fired.

Too late though, too late for Squirrel.

As the time all sped up and slowed, Golden's bullet dragged through Squirrel's shirt and into his belly.

He fell to the ground, flat on his back, didn't move, arms and legs all akimbo.

I urged Horse to our right to crush Golden between the other horses, but he moved too quick. He leaped forward, away from the panicking animals — *and the rawhide strip holding Horse to them finally broke, but we stayed where we were* — Golden already had hold of Eliza, spun her round in front of himself as a shield, so Rollins wouldn't risk shooting at him.

"Squirrel," she cried, and she squealed and screamed. But no matter how violent she squirmed, he held her tight as a drum-skin.

Her screams died away in her throat and turned now to sobs, as we looked down at Squirrel. Eyes open, unmoving he was, all undone on the ground, as the blood spread over his shirt like a slow-blooming flower.

Squirrel Prewitt was gutshot.

"Let her go, Luke," I said. "You know Rollins could shoot her! I know you care for the girl."

"Shut up, Frakes, you've caused enough trouble already. Squirrel's death is *your* doing, he used to do what he was told before he met you."

"Squirrel," the girl sobbed. "Oh, Squirrel."

The fight was all gone from her now.

It was a standoff alright. Luke Golden would not see Sam Rollins in the trees, not unless Rollins fired — but neither could Sam shoot at Golden, for the girl would likely be killed.

And me, I was still tied and more-or-less useless. *Except for Horse being free now.*

I glanced down at Squirrel, spent a few moments summing things up. *Is he still breathing?* I was sure I saw movement, his chest slowly rising and falling. He was gutshot, but he was alive — for how long, who could know? That depended first on one main thing — what the bullet had hit.

But also, he was still bleeding. He sure wouldn't live if all this took too much time.

"Luke, let *me* speak to Rollins," I said.

I thought he might shoot me for speaking, and hoped Horse would jump fast enough if the gun moved toward us — but Golden did not look around, and only said, "Why?"

He kept hold of the girl with his left arm as he watched for movement — some clue in the trees, near where he'd heard Rollins's voice.

"He'll listen to me, Luke, I'll tell him to leave. You can leave here alone, try to get away, go into hiding. You don't have much choice."

He laughed at me then, wholehearted and bitter. "You'd try anything, old man. I'm the one holding all of the Aces. You know that, well as I do."

"You're wrong, son," I said. "Young Squirrel lied to you, remember? That means my wife and daughter made it to the Spanish ranch on the mountain, and those men will come. They won't care about Eliza, they'll shoot you down right where you stand, if you're still here."

"I'm a U.S. damn Marshal," he cried. "People believe what I say! I can *do* whatever I want! I can kill anyone, then decide on a good reason later. You're a stupid old man, that's all you are, you don't know a thing."

"You're probably right," I replied. "But them Spanish fellers ain't like us — they don't care much for lawmen, you see. Not American ones. And you can't arrest them once you're dead — and you're all alone out here now, if you get my point, son. You killed all your allies."

I had edged Horse away from the others to give him some room, just in case we might need it.

"Speak again, Frakes, and I'll kill you," he said, as the spittle flew from his mouth. Then more quietly he added, "Then again, you'll make a good hostage, if I can't kill your fat little friend."

"Alright," I said. "But I warned you. And I doubt your girl's gonna care for you now, not now you killed her brother in front a'her eyes."

"Squirrel," she sobbed, choking hard on the word.

"Shut up," Golden growled. Then louder he called, "Town Marshal Rollins! *Sam?* I got a proposition for you."

Sam was clever enough not to answer. Stayed behind whatever tree he was at, and did not point his rifle yet either.

"One way or another," Luke called, "I'll be leaving here in one piece. You can die if you really want to, and Frakes will die too. And later, when this quiets down, I'll come for your families, I promise you that. But it doesn't have to *be* that way, does it? I killed all the Prewitts, and Simms is gone too. I have every dollar we've made as a gang. Half for you, half for me, Sam. That's twelve-thousand apiece. How much do they pay *you* for law work? Five-hundred a year? Maybe six?"

He waited a moment or two, but Rollins stayed silent.

"Twenty years pay, Samuel Rollins. You'll have it an hour from now, you just think about all that money. And with Simms outta the way, we can credit *you* with killin' the Prewitts, and you'll win the election next month, become County Sheriff. Oh, the money we'll make then — you and me, Samuel Rollins. Just come with me into town, the money's waiting for us right there — hidden in a safe place where no-one can find it."

"What about Frakes?" Rollins called.

You damn fool, I thought.

I could tell where he was, which tree he was behind — and that meant Golden could too. He was aimed to the left of it now, there weren't no doubt about it.

"I have just one condition," called Golden. "You'll let me arrest Frakes for murdering Simms, and go along with my story. That's all, Sam, what do you say? I just want Frakes to pay for what he did to my family."

"Squirrel," sobbed poor Eliza.

"Sam? You got ten seconds, then I'm gonna shoot Frakes, then kill you. You know you can't beat me anyway, I'm the best that there is. And even if you shoot Eliza, I'll see where the flash is, and I'll get to the cover of these horses. You'll die for no reason, Sam. Twelve-thousand dollars — *plus* the lives of your children."

"That's what you told Sheriff Simms," cried Eliza, top of her lungs.

And just like they say in the classics, *that's when all hell broke loose*.

Time moving more slow than fast—

A flash in the trees from Rollins's rifle—

Eliza gets thrown out the way—

Golden fires at the flash and he rolls as he fires, fires at Rollins again and again—

And Horse charges forward, rears high, comes down hard on Luke's skull with his great stamping feet—

The sweetest horse I ever knew raises a battlecry, stomping and stomping through Golden's pitiful screaming, again and again as I somehow stay on—

And somewhere below me, the sick-sound crack of a skull — that terrible noise unmistakeable— like a Christmas glass bauble that shatters, but evermuch bigger, a sound that's all horror. A sound you can never forget, if ever you heard it.

In a moment, so horribly broken, he is finally at peace in his death. And the formerly handsome Luke Golden stops lying — stops lying to himself *and* to others — and ceases to seek his revenge.

CHAPTER 39
BRANDY & HOPE

F irst, I had to calm Horse. That done, I called Rollins over, as I went straight to Squirrel.

Still breathing and yes, still unconscious — but maybe, just maybe, asleep.

Can't stand pain, and only passed out, like that day I first met him.

That was my hope.

"Eliza, bring the water," I said, as Rollins cut the ropes from my hands. Then I flexed them a little to get back some movement as I told her, "Young Squirrel's alive, but we gotta act quick."

With Rollins's help, I moved the boy onto his side, and looked at his back. The bullet had passed all the way through.

"You got any alcohol, Rollins?"

"I don't actually drink, Lyle," he said, apologetic. "I never thought about—"

"In Luke's saddlebags," said Eliza. "There's brandy."

"That'll sure do."

Sam Rollins told me then that my girls were just fine — though unhappy they'd not been allowed to come here to *"help."*

Squirrel had sent them along a back trail he knew — just an animal track it was really. And that one led to another that led to John Williamson's place, more-or-less.

They'll be waiting there for me.

"Turns out the Prewitts have been here two weeks," Rollins said. "And Squirrel knows all the trails better than I do."

As I took off Horse's saddle to prop up Squirrel's head with, I said, "Nice shooting at the end, Sam."

"But I fired into the air."

"That's what I mean," I said. "It was the only right shot you could take. If you'd fired again, you coulda killed me or Horse."

"You did warn me not to shoot Horse — that's about *all* you told me."

He lifted Squirrel's head while I put the saddle in underneath, and we got him propped up right. Then we left Eliza with him a minute, cooling his face some with a damp cloth.

"You done good, Sam Rollins," I told him. "You're a man I'd ride the river with anytime. I'm sorry I misjudged you, it won't happen again."

He nodded, that was all, didn't speak.

It was enough.

We was friends now.

I sent him to fetch a doctor from Los Angeles then,

right away. Woulda took too long to drag Squirrel there on a travois[1], and in his state, it coulda killed him.

Before Rollins left, he covered Luke's head with one a'my saddle blankets — I use two on Horse these days.

Me and Eliza cleaned the wound best we could from both sides. I tore some of the lining outta my coat to plug up the bullet holes with, stop it bleeding too much. For a girl who had really been through it these terrible hours, she never stopped trying.

I admired her, I really did.

It had been a long day. A REAL long day.

While we waited for the Doc, Squirrel slept. He never even woke when we poured brandy into his wounds. Eyes fluttered a little, and his body tensed some as he groaned, but that's all it was.

There being not much else to do, me and Eliza, we talked some. Drank about a snifter's worth of that top-shelf brandy — maybe two snifters' worth — to settle our nerves.

That poor girl told me things that turned my hair grayer in an instant. It's true, I ain't makin' this up — when I looked in the mirror next morning, I was some degrees grayer than I'd been before. My beard was coming back too, which feels good somehow, though it itches me some — guess I'll let it grow back now, and be me again, all the way through.

One a'them things Eliza told me was of how she met young Luke Golden. Not easy for her to tell it, but it seemed like she needed to do so right then. Get it off her chest somehow, the heavy weight of it.

It was after Luke and his partner took her and one of

her skunk brothers prisoner, and dragged 'em back to the hoosegow in Colorado Springs.

The story Luke Golden had told me about it was lies — like most everything else he said. It had actually been Eliza, not her brother Jimmy, who wanted to co-operate with the Law, so she could get all her murderous brothers arrested. Not Squirrel, a'course — same as her, he was never really part of the gang. They just weren't allowed to leave. The others used them as slaves.

And that weren't the worst of it.

---

1. TRAVOIS: A type of sledge made from two joined poles, and pulled by a horse, mule or dog. Native Americans used them to carry their goods, but they're also useful for bodies, dead or alive.

CHAPTER 40
A HARD TRUTH TO HEAR

Truth of it was, young Squirrel was the only reason Eliza had been here with her brothers.

Three years back, she had been sent away east to a pretty good school by her mother — and was getting a fine education. The woman sent Eliza to that school soon as her mean husband died, but there was only enough money to send one of 'em, so Squirrel stayed home. If you're slow like I was, you won't have worked it out yet — but Eliza and Squirrel had a different mother than all the older boys.

No wonder they looked and acted so different. I shoulda realized that. You got sloppy, Lyle, too much a'the easy life this past year, lookin' out at that big salty ocean, the endlessness of it.

Problem was, she went home for the burial when her dear mother died — and them older skunk brothers told her they'd kill Squirrel if ever she left 'em. Beat the pair of 'em senseless when they tried it once, too.

They hit the Owl Hoot Trail after that, killing and raping and thieving. But a real top pair of young lawmen came along, and that's how she met young Luke.

So here's how it went at the hoosegow in Colorado Springs: Luke Golden's partner died later that night from the wounds he got during the shootout — and when Eliza told Luke she was a Prewitt, his ears had pricked up like a dog's when it sees a choice bone. She told him she could lead him to their hideout, and give accounts of all the things they had told her, as well as a few things she'd seen for herself that would lock them skunks up for years.

But that weren't what Luke wanted.

Oh, he wrote her information down alright. Then he left and said he'd come back in the morning. But three hours later, in the dead of the night he was back. Walked in calm as you like and cut the throat of the night guard — *who he SAID was a very bad man, a molester of children —* then he knocked out Jimmy Prewitt with ether, before tying him up, cutting off most of his fingers, and knocking out most of his teeth before they left the cell.

Then he strung Jimmy up just outside the town border — hung him up by his reproductive parts, was how Eliza put it — and left him there to die a slow death while they rode to a hideout Luke knew of nearby.

Hanging Jimmy by those parts was because of what that low skunk had done to Eliza — she'd admitted to Luke that Jimmy had used her that way. It was why her dear mother had sent her to school in the first place.

Terrible thing.

Eliza cried like a little girl when she told me, and I said,

"Sure you don't wish to stop, girl? It's alright if you stop, you been through it alright — but I'll listen if you wish to talk. It's up to you."

She told me it felt better to have finally said it to someone other than Luke — and she said she wished to go on, tell me more of what happened.

They did *not* go to see the other Prewitts right away. No, the handsome young Luke took his time, gentled the girl into believing he was a good man, despite what he'd just done to those *"bad ones."*

Made love to her on the *second* night, she told me — she whispered it like it was sinful and said, "It was wicked of me I know. He *had* killed my brother. I'm sorry, Mister Frakes."

I told her she didn't have cause to say sorry to no one. Told her too, that love's strange when you're young — *and it don't get less strange when you're older, just for the record*.

But what she went through, I explained, it was no wonder she fell for young Luke. "He promised to save you, and save Squirrel too. And you knew he'd protect you, I guess, after what he done to Jimmy. And one more thing I must say — Jimmy deserved it."

Musta took some huge stones, for Luke Golden to ride into that hideout after what he'd just done to their brother.

But he'd promised Eliza it was step one to saving young Squirrel — and that it would take time. Told her he would rid her of all her half-brothers, if she'd only trust him to do it in his own way.

And also, he told her he loved her.

When he finally rode into their hideout, he told 'em he

had a great reason to be there, and that he'd make 'em all rich besides — told 'em then how he and them had a mutual enemy, the man who had murdered their cousins, Lyle damn Frakes. And he told them ugly Prewitts that it had been *Jimmy* who skunked 'em all out. Said Jimmy had listed their crimes and told Luke where they were, in exchange for a light sentence — instead of him being strung up for killing Luke's partner, a loved and respected United States Deputy Marshal.

'Jimmy said we should pin it on Frank,' was what Golden told them.

Upshot was, they believed him. No one touched Eliza in wrong ways again, and it seemed like Luke Golden loved her. He told them he'd just found out where Lyle Frakes was, and told them he had a plan — a plan that would bring them revenge, and riches as well.

"I believed him," she said. "Even when he told me to go kidnap Mary, and said that she would not be harmed, and neither would you."

"But hadn't he always *said* that he wanted to kill me?"

"Not in private, Mister Frakes. He told *me* that you were a friend of his father's. Imagine? That's irony too, I suppose."

"One word for it, I guess. Better word is a *lie.*"

"Luke told me that even if he jailed my brothers, they'd find a way to break out, and maybe they'd find us. Perhaps even kill Squirrel. And he said when we came here, that you'd declined to help him get rid of my half-brothers. But he said that he needed you there so they'd let down their guard — and he and Sheriff Simms would do what was needed. He said it was the only way, Mister Frakes. On that point, I think Luke was right. Before now, they've always been wary of Luke."

The whole time we'd talked, we had tried to keep Squirrel comfortable, mopping his brow with a cool wet kerchief.

The bleeding had stopped a good while and a moon had appeared, enough to light the Doc's way. He and Rollins would not be much longer.

"You're a good girl, Eliza," I told her. "You got hornswoggled[1] by a man, and you sure ain't the first girl that's happened to."

I was watching young Squirrel close. Thought his eyes was moving around some, in behind his eyelids.

Good sign I hope. Sometimes it's a bad one.

"He never did love me, did he, Mister Frakes? I'm a fool, I've been such a—"

"Oh, but he did, Miss Eliza," I said, and I hoped I was making it sound like the truth. "It was hard for Luke at the end here, when the noose closed in on him. And yet, when the shootin' got started, he threw you clear. He loved you alright. He was a muddled up man, but the one thing I know for sure is, he loved you."

"Well," she said. "I love my dear brother here more than I could love *any* other man."

"What's Squirrel's *real* name, Miss Eliza? If you don't mind me asking."

"Oh," she said. "Oh, we can call him by that now again. My half-brothers forbade it, you see. His real name is Sallie!"

"Don't call me that, Sis," came a hoarse voice from between us. Then he looked up at me and said, "Just Squirrel, please, Mister Frakes! Don't tell no one I got a girl's name."

"Squirrel!" she finally cried as she gripped both his cheeks, and the tears of relief poured out her eyes. "You're okay, you're really okay!"

And I breathed a great sigh of relief, for I knew then he would be.

---

1. HORNSWOGGLED: To be tricked or cheated, have the wool pulled over your eyes. Also known as Gulled.

CHAPTER 41
RICHES

A month later, we was all sitting out on the porch, enjoying a Saturday lunch.

Funny thing, I thought then. *Ain't that how this story got started?*

Difference now was, instead a'young Squirrel preparing to charge at our home like as if he would kill us, he's more-or-less part a'the family.

He was sat there drinking his tea, and trying not to laugh at one of old Dot Rollins's stories — guess I shouldn't call her old, she's likely younger'n I am. But you know, the word *old* ain't an insult. It means a whole lotta good things, and we should celebrate them things more than we do.

Anyway, it still hurts young Squirrel to laugh, but his wounds is all healing good as might be expected. Somehow that bullet mostly missed all things important — nicked one part of his insides that mattered, some funny name. Appendixes, I think the Doc said — anyway, he cut the thing out. Reckoned folks don't need that part anyway, which raises more questions than answers, but he's a good Doc. So if that's what he reckons, I reckon it's all fine by me. And *that* operation was just one extra scar — Squirrel rated it better than dying.

Things took a little sorting out that first few days. That one surviving Deputy, the feller Simms *said* had high-tailed it at the first sign of trouble, had actually been sent away east by Simms, to hunt for some feller who never even existed. He was gone two more days, and by then the Federal Marshal's Office had sent a senior man in to sort it all out.

At first that feller wanted to lock Squirrel back up, and Eliza too. But I had a little sway with him, on account of him being a cousin of my former partner — *good ol' Shotgun Bill Bryden* — back when we two worked as Federal Deputies.

Rollins and me told our stories, then Marshal Tom Bryden deputized the both of us — just temporary — so we could help sort it all out. Led to a mountain of damn paperwork we had to do, but it was eventually worth it. They let Squirrel and Eliza go free, just like they should.

So now here we were, all out on the porch, with the sound of the crashing waves for our music, and each other's company for riches.

Yes, we sure have some riches.

Speaking of riches, Eliza knew Luke Golden well enough to find where the twenty-four thousand was hid — though she weren't allowed to keep it, a'course.

They called it Government Property. Funny how when citizens steal, they get locked up for it — but when the

Government 'recover' the money, they reckon *they* earned it square.

Turned out too, that Luke Golden also had paperwork hidden away — papers which would have been enough for Eliza and Squirrel and himself to start up new lives under different names.

He really did love her, I guess. When I'd told her he did, just after he died, I hadn't really believed it. I just figured she needed to hear it right at that moment.

Proves no one's ALL bad, I guess — even the most hateful and meanest of skunks can truly love someone else. Yessir, love can be strange, like I told you before.

Speaking of which, a striking development, that might should change things round here soon: I had not noticed this myself, but Georgina mentioned it to me this morning, before Rollins and his mother and his children arrived for our weekly luncheon together — and now I paid attention, it was plain as the nose on my old (and again bearded) face. Sam Rollins and Eliza have eyes for each other.

Georgina said it hadn't happened right away — but since everything settled down, and Eliza and Squirrel came here to live with us, the whole thing just sorta blossomed.

Well, good luck to 'em both.

As for Mary, she's sorta smitten with Squirrel — in a ten-year-old-girl sorta way. I don't think he notices, and she'll move onto someone else soon, I'd probably reckon. Well, it's harmless for now, but I'll be gettin' watchful within a couple more years. Problem is, that girl seems to be always smitten with *someone*. Even the likes of Luke Golden.

We don't talk about him much no more.

But when we did talk about him, we worked somethin' out. Which was that Luke Golden coulda been a great lawman, and perhaps a great man in all sorts a'ways — if only he'd kept being *who* he was in the first place.

Back before his father went wrong, he had been a fine boy, by every account.

But that kid back then — whose dear mother had been so rightly concerned for — well, that kid died long ago, that's the tragedy of it. Poor Ricky Bellow died one little piece at a time, eaten up by his rage and revengeful desires. And I reckon seeing all that, was what *really* killed his poor Ma.

Two other things me and Georgina *did* speak of together, related to all these events:

First thing, we agreed my instincts was rusty, on account of too much easy living.

"Then again," Georgina pointed out, "you mistrusted Luke Golden at first, even though he had everyone else wrapped 'round his fingers. That alone proves you've still *mostly* got it. *And* you also trusted Squirrel — and *he* was supposedly an outlaw. We just need to trust you, Kit, let you make the important decisions."

"Guess you're right, Princess, when you put it like that. I'll try to make them decisions all good ones, now on."

"You'll need a *little* help with that, of course," she added with a chuckle, before kissing me like I deserved it.

And the *second thing* we spoke of, well, that was something I'd never made one inch of progress with before.

Georgina agreed now, that I *should* teach she and Mary to shoot.

And we've already started.

Thing about that is, Mary was an absolute natural from the very first day. Coulda shot the stinger off of a bee, if they made bullets right size for that. But some folks ain't naturals at all, and it averages out.

No other way to say it than the truth I guess — as good as Mary was, Georgina was equally bad. This surprised me no end, and I figured she was doing it on purpose, at least to begin with. But even when I tried to bribe her with a shopping expedition — thousand dollar stake — she could not hit a man-sized target from twenty feet away. Not even with Gertrude.

And Gertrude don't even NEED human help, most circumstances. Even Dot Rollins hit the target — with Gertrude's help a'course — and ol' Dot had never fired a single dang bullet before.

Might need to try Georgina out on a scattergun, I reckon. Though I wouldn't wish to be standing too close when she tries it.

Let's just say, Georgina's the best rider I ever seen sit a horse, and that such gifts have to be paid for in some other way — it averages out in the end, I guess, my main meaning.

And I never actually *tell* her that she's the worst shot I ever saw in all my long years. I've seen blind men shoot better'n she does.

So I'm sitting here now with all a'these riches around me — family, friends, good food and mighty fine horses.

And a'course, our nice little ranch by the sea, with a comfortable home built to suit all our needs.

We'd be loco ever to leave it.

But maybe that's just what we are.

See, here's the thing. I got this letter burning a hole in my pocket, and ain't mentioned it yet, except to Georgina. Letter was sent to my by a good friend, a Deputy Marshal who helped me to save Mary's life, back in Cheyenne a year ago at the orphanage. Well, we all saved each other's lives I guess — I surely know Mary saved mine.

The letter is simple enough, and here's what it says:

Dear Lyle

Thank you for your recent letter. As you suspected, I had indeed written to you about Luke Golden. And yes, the letter contained a warning about him. He was clever, but asking too many questions about you and your time in Cheyenne.

Please note, I ALSO sent you a telegram. Whether those two correspondences were apprehended here or there, I don't know. But you may wish to speak to folks there — as I did here — of dire consequences if it ever happens again.

We were happy to hear you all survived the visit from that rotten apple and his murderous gang. Also, that you were able to rescue the girl and her brother — and of course, your dear Mary. Yes, I know your letter said that you didn't play much of a part in their rescue, but I've read the official reports, and know what the truth is.

But even before that, my dear old dad read a

newspaper report, and assured me the whole thing had Lyle Frakes written all over it.

'Tough as old boots, Lyle Frakes,' that's what he said. Reckon I heard that six-hundred times now. Maybe seven. He still likes to say it, and I'll never argue the point.

Anyway, while ever my old dad keeps saying it, I'll know his brain's working just fine.

I guess you changing your name for a year didn't change your stars like I said it would. And now you're back in the news, there will likely be others come after you. I would suggest you change your name once again, but I know what you'd say about that.

I KNOW you've missed all the action. My old man told me he was surprised you stayed quiet a whole year. I hope one day he gets to meet you in person — he'd like that, and I think you'd like him.

Well, that was the first sheet of paper. Georgina wants me to read the other sheet out, right here and now, while our good friends are here. She believes it'll be easier for Mary if they're all here when she gets the news. The child sees old Dot Rollins like a sorta grandmother I guess — and as for Eliza, she and Mary are close as two sisters.

"Listen up, everyone," I tell them, and they all quiet down. "I got a letter to read out, then decisions to make which affect every one of us. And while it's up to Mary most of all, I value all of your opinions."

And I take out the letter from my pocket, and the little eyeglasses I wear now to read with.

CHAPTER 42
JUSTICE & TRUTH

Funny thing. At every important moment, ol' Horse seems to sense it, comes over and gets himself involved. Did so each time his foals was born — a colt and two fillies they are — all in this past month. He seems to approve of all three, and I reckon he's a fair judge of horseflesh.

I won't go into the names Mary gave them three foals, at least not for the moment. Let's just say I hope she forgets what she called 'em, or changes her mind. Me, I call 'em Colt, Filly and Young'Un.

Anyway, soon as I put on my glasses and took out the letter, Horse's big lovely head was right there, looking over my shoulder. Seemed like his plan was to read it. Least he don't need glasses.

"Get out of that, you old pest," cried Georgina, as everyone laughed.

Well, it's one thing to give Horse an order and another thing to enforce it. He weren't nohow impressed with being shut out, so he closed his lips over the letter and attempted to thieve it.

"Give it up," I said, slapping the side of his face some, "I need that, you stealin' skunk."

Amid all the laughter, Mary bribed the equine busybody to give up the letter, in exchange for a fresh-baked biscuit she'd just buttered and took a small bite from.

Considering that a fair trade, Horse consented to leave, but he didn't go far — stood about listening, he did, from a few yards away. You'd think that nice gentle breeze and warm sun would be enough, but not for ol' Horse — he's gotta be in on everything, including decisions for our future.

"Alright, just so you all know," I announced, once the busybody stopped all his chewing and chomping. "This letter is from a good friend of ours, a Deputy who works in Cheyenne."

"Mister Emmett!" said Mary, and she gripped Eliza's arm with excitement. "He's *such* a nice man"

"That's right, Mary," said Georgina, from Mary's other side. "It's from Deputy Emmett Slaughter. Now hush while your father reads it out, and let's not interrupt him before he gets through it."

Horse rested his head on my shoulder — I guess he can read now, or wants me to think so — then I cleared my throat and began.

"I have news that will interest you, Lyle.

A man I arrested yesterday after a shootout made a deathbed confession. He was gutshot, and knew he was dying, so offered me this information in exchange for me placing a loaded pistol into his hand, so he could end his own suffering.

You might imagine how my ears pricked up when he mentioned the murder of a married couple named Wilson, nearby to here two years ago. Yes, your own Mary's parents."

I watched Mary as I read it out. Her eyes gleamed dark and intense when I said it, and she nodded for me to continue.

I nodded back, and went on.

"Now before you get TOO excited, Lyle, the man died a few seconds later. Not a thing I could do. And all I really got from him was the name of the man who had actually pulled the trigger to kill Mary's folks. If this dying man hadn't spent so long explaining his own innocence of it, I might have got something more from him.

Hard to get words from a dead man.

The name he gave me has been no help to me yet. Like I said, it was only twelve hours ago, and I've been asleep four of those.

The man who died was Red Abbott. He was in a bad way, not making sense half the time, but he told me the shootist's name was Jesse Gillespie.

Please keep the name quiet for now — I'll explain all that soon. We have to tread carefully here.

I'll write you as soon as I find something useful.
With friendship and greatest respect
Emmett Slaughter
Cheyenne."

If Mary's eyes gleamed before, now they actually burned. Burned with purpose. For all it's intenseness, her face showed no trace of hatred — but instead, a desire for justice.

Justice and Truth.

Them ten-year-old eyes a'hers burned into mine, and it shocked me, the ancientness of 'em. I had never quite noticed before, but they was the eyes of what some people call an *'old soul.'* And for all of her youth and her lovely, childlike ways, she seemed ancient and wise to me now.

For several moments she looked to her mother, not speaking, but it *was* conversation — then she turned back to me, and she smiled, ever so slightly.

And she only said, "When do we leave?"

And just like that, it was decided.

We would go to Cheyenne.

The End

THE DERRINGER

If seven-year-old Roy Stone had done what his Ma told him to, he'd never have known the truth of what happened at all.

He'd never have seen the double-cross, never have witnessed the murders, never seen the killer's blowed-apart finger. But the poor kid saw the whole rotten thing, and watched his mother die on the floor.

"I'm going to kill you," little Roy cried at the killer – but Big Jim only laughed with contempt.

But that little boy meant what he said – and what's more, he believed it.

He would grow up and kill that big man. That was all that now mattered.

Available as an eBook and in paperback.

WOLF TOWN

Cleve Lawson is a man for minding his business. But when he witnesses a stranger murdered by road agents, then the outlaws kill his best friend, Cleve decides it's high time he stuck his nose in where it don't belong.

As if all that ain't problems enough, he meets a tough yet beautiful woman who takes a shine to him – and a feller with fists of iron who takes unkindly to that.

Throw in a murderous road agent gone loco, an unfaithful dog, a wise-cracking Sheriff, and a range war between sheep and cattle men, and Cleve's got more troubles than an unarmed man in the middle of a gunfight.

Available as an eBook and in paperback.

FYRE

What if you went off to fight for what's right, and someone told your sweetheart you'd died? What if that same person told you that she was dead too?

What if that man up and married her? After secretly killing her family? And what if that man was the brother you trusted?

And what if, one day, you came home?

A story of trickery and cunning, of brotherhood and truth, and of war. Of bandits and shootouts and justice, and of doing what's right. Of a tall man who slithered, and a dwarf who stood tall as the clouds, and became Billy's friend.

It's the story of how Billy Ray becomes Billy Fyre – and how, seven long years after being told he'd lost everything, finally, Billy comes home, to fight for what's his.

Available as an eBook and in paperback.

WILDCAT CREEK

Toy Gooden always did think the best of the people he knew – that's how his troubles all started, and just kept on getting bigger.

When ten-year-old Toy takes the blame for a killing done by his best friend, it sets off a chain of events that's a never-ending passel of trouble.

Ten years on, wanted for a robbery and murder he didn't commit, and hated by his whole home town, Toy has to save Wildcat Creek (those very folks) from the bloodthirsty Gilman Gang. With no other help than a meddlesome twelve-year-old orphan, an ancient decrepit doctor, and a pesky tomboy outlaw who keeps insisting she wants to marry him, looks like Toy's got more troubles than a fingerless man in a gunfight.

Available as an eBook and in paperback.

.

Printed in Great Britain
by Amazon